The Incorruptible Ivy Jackson and the Museum Murder

THE INCORRUPTIBLE IVY JACKSON MYSTERIES
BOOK 1

ROSIE A. POINT

The Incorruptible Ivy Jackson and the Museum Murder
The Incorruptible Ivy Jackson Mysteries Book 1

Copyright © 2023 by Rosie A. Point.

www.rosiepointbooks.com

Cover by DLR Cover Designs
www.dlrcoverdesigns.com

You're invited!

Hi there, reader!

I'd like to formally invite you to join my awesome community of readers. We love to chat about cozy mysteries, cooking, and pets.

It's super fun because I get to share chapters from yet-to-be-released books, fun recipes, pictures, and do giveaways with the people who enjoy my stories the most.

So whether you're a new reader or you've been enjoying my stories for a while, you can catch up with other like-minded readers, and get lots of cool content by visiting my website at *www.rosiepointbooks.com* and signing up for my mailing list.

Or simply search for me on *www.bookbub.com* and follow me there.

I look forward to getting to know you better.

Let's get into the story!

Yours,
Rosie

One

The murder that took place during early spring in Somewhere, Ohio, would have shaken the community to its core if not for the fact that the small town, my hometown, was already in a downward spiral.

There had been a steady descent into crime for years, even prior to my husband's passing, but my natural instinct was to delineate the time before and after Darren's death. So far, things seemed a heck of a lot worse after his passing.

I have taken some comfort in creating timelines out of the madness that took place this spring.

It started on a cool morning, during my walk through Rothstar, the suburb that held our old family home.

"Almost there, Boo." I held the end of his blue leash in one hand, the other clutching the curved handle of my umbrella. The weatherman had suggested rain this morning, but I wasn't about to let that ruin our walk.

It was my birthday, and I had gotten into the habit of trying to celebrate it again—a chore that had become difficult after losing Darren.

Boo, my sassy border collie, barked an excited response, his paws tapping along the concrete sidewalk. He occasionally stopped to sniff grass blades peeking beneath picket fences or to lift his leg at a mailbox or fire hydrant.

I inhaled the cool air, my heart beating out a pattern I didn't enjoy.

"Just around the corner," I said softly.

A muted bark from Boo.

The houses in Rothstar were double-story, most of them well-kept, but even in the middle-class suburbs of Somewhere, the rot had started to take hold. A slow degradation had befallen the town ever since the old plastics factory had closed and the money had left with it.

We turned the corner, and the house came into view.

"There it is," I said, my voice cracking.

I clicked my tongue at myself. Silly to be so sentimental, but this was part of our walking route. The old house. Our old house.

"You never knew this place, Boo," I said, stopping outside the gate, which hung skew on its hinges. "But you would have loved it."

With its gabled roof, the double-story home still had a warm atmosphere, even though it was abandoned. The first-floor windows had been shattered, and the front door was slightly ajar, but if I closed my eyes, I could go back in time and remember...

The soft laughter of my children running around the old oak tree, playing. Darren's hammering, building them the tree house. The distant slam of a door or the scrape of chairs as we all sat down for dinner at the table.

I opened my eyes, shaking my head at myself, tears welling and threatening to spill over.

Boo licked my calf, his tongue pulling on the pair of stockings I'd chosen this morning—bright purple to suit my bowler hat.

I bent and petted his soft forehead right where the white fur had created a heart on his crown.

"You're a blessing," I said.

Boo barked and jumped to his paws, then darted off toward the end of the road, trailing the end of his leash. My hand was still outstretched, mid-stroke.

"Did I say blessing?" I muttered. "I meant curse."

I'd have bet my bowler hat that Boo had caught a whiff of another dog. He was absolutely obsessed with making friends or terrorizing—mutually inclusive in most cases—every dog in Somewhere.

"Get back here, Boo!" I called, hurrying away from the

house. "Get back here!" I chased after him as fast as my aching hip could take me, the end of my umbrella rapping against the sidewalk, my other hand holding my bowler hat to my gray curls.

The darn dog would be the death of me. That or he was rapidly increasing my cardio fitness and lengthening my life.

I reached the corner and found Boo there, his hackles raised, growling at something just out of sight.

"What is—?"

I peered down the adjacent street, and a cold flush rushed over my skin.

A woman, she had to be about the same age as my daughter—in her thirties—was pressed against a gnarled tree that flanked the road. A man pressed his hand to her throat and searched her pockets. Robbing her.

The victim didn't yelp or shriek but held perfectly still, pale as a sheet.

"Sic him," I said to Boo. "I'm right behind you."

Boo launched down the street, a silent black and white arrow aimed at a target. I followed, forgetting my hip, and broke into a trot, clasping my umbrella in both hands.

The thief wore a black mask and looked up, the whites of his eyes showing as Boo collided with his leg. A feral yell followed the collision as Boo dug his teeth into the man's ankle and started yanking and shaking like the mugger was a chew toy.

"Atta boy," I said as I arrived on the scene.

I double-fisted the end of my umbrella and swung it around. The resounding crack of the umbrella striking the man's jaw gave me just a breath of satisfaction. I continued swinging, and Boo continued biting and shaking.

The man's screams became effeminate. The victim of the attack stood stock still, in shock, as we unleashed our fury on the man.

The thief's sensory overload wouldn't last long, and when he got past it, he would start a counter-attack. I wasn't oblivious to the fact that I was an *old woman* and would probably crumple like an origami duck if he took a swing at me.

"Call the police," I said to the woman between swings.

The word "police" awoke something in the attacker. He managed to shake Boo free—or maybe Boo sensed it was time to let him go—and made a run for it down the road, trailing the end of his tattered pants leg, blood, and a serious lack of dignity.

"And don't come back!" I shook my umbrella.

Boo barked and started after him, but I whistled him back. Border collies were on the smaller side, and that thief wouldn't be taken by surprise twice in the span of a few minutes.

The woman gave a shuddering gasp, and I took her by the arm carefully, bringing her away from the tree. "Do you live nearby?" I asked.

She pointed up toward the house on the opposite side of the street. "O-Over there."

"Perhaps you should go home and have something sweet to drink before you report this to the police. We can come with you, if you'd like," I said.

"Thank you," she whispered. "I—You saved me."

"It was mostly Boo."

My dog gave a happy bark, and the woman jerked a little at the noise. Her facial features softened into a pretty smile. "Thank you, Boo," she said. "That's a funny name."

We helped the woman across the road and waited patiently as she unlocked the front door with trembling hands. "Y-You have to come in," she said. "Please. I don't know how I can repay you for this."

"No need to repay us," I said. "Though, Boo looks like he needs a bowl of water if you've got one."

The woman led us into a neatly kept home with pictures on the walls—she was married, it seemed, but no children. Her kitchen was lemon yellow and smelled faintly of detergent. A takeout menu from the local pizza place was stuck to the fridge under an "I heart NYC" magnet.

"New to town?" I asked.

She nodded. "I'm Melanie."

"Ivy," I said, "Ivy Jackson. I'm sorry about the poor introduction to the town. Somewhere was a lot friendlier in the past."

Melanie didn't say anything but set about fixing a pot of coffee and getting Boo a bowl of water. The poor woman was shaken up, and she reminded me of my daughter, Brianna—though she was blonde and pale, where Brianna was raven-haired and had an even darker complexion than me. Maybe it was the attitude—a sweetness that I missed—that reminded me of Bri. Or maybe it was that I hadn't seen my daughter since her father's funeral.

A tiny pill of discomfort lodged itself in my chest then, and I determined that I wouldn't stop at anything to clean up this town if it meant I could bring things back to the way they were meant to be.

Two

That afternoon, I brought the cake out of the oven and allowed it to cool on the silver racks I had bought from a bakery wholesaler in Cincinnati when Darren and I were on vacation. My cottage, removed from the town by a dirt road, was small, cozy, and hidden between trees that flanked a farmer's field. Boo had plenty of room to run and play, which was exactly what he'd done since we'd arrived home from our morning walk.

I rested my palms on the granite countertop, either side of the rack, and frowned at the cake.

Chocolate cake. My favorite. And I had already prepared a ganache to go over the top, with buttercream for the middle.

I would cut it up and share it with my only friend, Miriam, at the library and my new neighbor, two cottages down the road, so she could form an opinion of me that didn't reflect what most townsfolk thought. That I was a grumpy old hermit who lived in the woods with her uncontrollable dog.

While the cake cooled, I sat in Darren's favorite recliner in the open-plan living room that led into the kitchen and picked up a worn copy of one of my favorite novels—*The Murder of Roger Ackroyd.*

My phone rang before I could start reading it for the umpteenth time, and I had to search around the living room until I found it underneath one of the sofa cushions.

Brianna's name flashed on the screen, and my heart swelled with joy.

"Bri!"

"Hello, Mom," she replied, the shrieks of one of my boisterous grandchildren punctuating her greeting. "Sorry, just a sec. Dewayne found a bag of flour—" There was a click as the line went dead.

I frowned, pulling the phone away from my ear. It rang a second time.

"Hello?"

"Disaster averted," Briana laughed. "We were baking cookies."

"That's nice," I said.

"Happy birthday, Mom!"

"Thank you, honey." I smiled, tears welling in my eyes.

"I walked past the old house today. You remember it, right?"

"Of course," Bri said. "I grew up there, Mom. How could I forget?"

"It's easy to forget things once they're out of sight. I haven't heard from your brother yet. Do you know if he's fine?"

"Owen's doing great. I talked to him yesterday. Think he's just busy. He mentioned a new job—I think he's changing airlines, but I'm not one hundred percent sure?" Brianna was interrupted by the thump of something, followed by a child wailing. "Dewayne! Come on, honey, what are you doing? Give me—Dewayne!"

Toddlers were both a joy and a trial. Brianna was getting a little payback for her childhood, was my guess.

"Bri?"

"I'm here," she said. "Barely. Why are boys so much more... boisterous than girls? Taniel never does this kind of thing. Flour and breaking into cabinets, uh."

I chuckled. "I miss you and the kids. Denzel too. You've got to visit sometime soon."

"After everything you've told me about the upswing in crime..."

"Oh, honey, that's just me being me," I said, trying not to feel guilty about the white lie. I was tired of not seeing my grandbabies and my children. They had busy lives, but at this point, I would *pay* for them to come visit. "It's getting safer by the day. Really, you should come!"

"I'll talk to Denzel about it," Bri said.

I'd have to take that as a maybe. "Great." But even as I said the word, my insides sank. "We could go by the old house. It's a good family home."

"I'm not moving into our family home, Mom," Bri said with a long-suffering sigh. "But I miss you too. Look, I'd better go. Taniel has gone quiet, and we both know what that means."

"Mischief."

"Happy birthday, Mom," Bri said. "I love you."

"I love you—" But Bri had already hung up.

I checked my phone and found a text message from my son, Owen.

"Hi, Mom! Happy Birthday! I just wanted to send a message real quick to tell you I love you. I'm about to fly, so I can't call, but I'll try to touch base later." It was followed by several of those heart emojis and one that looked like an explosion.

I set my phone on the coffee table and inhaled the silence, the Poirot novel resting face down in my lap. The loneliness crept up on me daily, clawing at me with memories, especially when Boo was out of the cottage, exploring in the woods or the field.

"Silly," I grunted, lifting my book again, then squinted

at the words when I realized I'd forgotten to put on my reading glasses.

Boo barreled through the doggy door and barked at me excitedly, his lower half brown with mud.

"What on earth? Where have you been this time?" I asked. "I hope you didn't break into someone's house again."

Boo had a bad habit of getting himself dirty and then tracking that dirt through other people's cottages. There were four cottages along my road, one abandoned, one that held a family who absolutely despised Boo, and the final one inhabited by the new neighbors.

Boo gave me another happy bark before plonking his dirty doggy butt on the wooden floorboards and scratching at his collar, flicking mud in every direction.

I laughed at his antics—I didn't mind cleaning, and he kept me young and busy.

The next hour was spent bathing Boo, then cleaning the house before moving on to the cake. The ganache was perfectly runny and rich, the buttercream just sugary enough. I cut up the finished product into neat slices, gave Boo a special doggy, chocolate-free cupcake I had bought from the local vet, and ate my piece of cake over the sink.

"Another year gone," I said, "and who knew sixty-seven would—"

My phone trilled on the coffee table, and I hurriedly

collected it, hoping it was Owen checking in. Instead, Miriam's name presented itself on my screen.

"Good afternoon, Mira," I said. "How—?"

"Ivy! You have to come quick!" Miriam was breathless. "To the library! Please. I need your help with something urgent."

"Are you okay? Do you need me to call the police?"

"No, no. They wouldn't do anything useful, anyway. I need you to come yourself. Before it's too late." The line went dead.

I grabbed Boo's leash, slipped on my comfortable sandals, and placed my bowler hat on my head before hurrying out the door.

Three

The Somewhere Public Library was located on the stretch of road that looped back into town. It wasn't a far walk along the looping dirt lane that wound past the cottages, and I found it necessary to take a quick pace, Boo jogging ahead, his leash trailing along in the dirt behind him. It was my practice to let him roam free out here, mostly because he loved nature, but partly because holding him back was hard on my joints.

The library was a recent addition to the town, sponsored by one of the wealthier families—the Stones—who had once owned the plastic factory that had shut down. Garrett Stone had sold the plastic factory five years ago—to the highest bidder. It was a pity that the bidder had opted to run the factory into the ground.

Many Somewhereians believed that the Stones were to

blame for the factory's closure, and the family tried to improve their poor public image by sponsoring the library and the museum in town.

A tone deaf move for the most part, since a lot of Somewhere's citizens were struggling to make ends meet and didn't have time to read or stroll around in a marble-columned building, oohing and aahing at exhibits that oftentimes had nothing to do with local Ohioan history.

Boo stopped at the intersection where the tar began, waiting for me to take hold of his leash, and we hurried toward the library—a brick building with hidden rooms and shelves galore.

"Miriam?" I called the minute we stepped through the open front doors. It was a pleasant afternoon, and the breeze carried a scent of peonies that mingled with the smell of old books, cracked spines, and turned pages. "Miriam, are you in here? Are you all right?"

The bang of books falling in the library brought a worried bark from Boo.

"Miriam!"

But there was no answer.

Boo and I headed between the shelves toward the sound of the commotion. Boo's wet, black nose sniffled this way and that, and he tugged on the end of his leash, guiding me left and then right until we found a hidden nook between the bookcases.

A reading area with tables and chairs, the table piled high with books.

"Miriam?"

A shriek came from behind the tower of books, and a set of bright green eyes, framed by round wire-rimmed glasses, peered over them at me. Miriam's speckled forehead, wrinkled with age like a well-read book, creased.

"Ivy! I thought you'd never get here."

Boo barked at her.

"Oh, hello, Boo." She came around the table, her hands behind her back. "You took your time to get here."

"We came as fast as we could." There was more to this than met the eye. "I thought you were in danger, the way you were talking on the phone."

"Danger?" Miriam gave a sly smile, tucking a curl of red hair behind one ear. "Moi? Never. But a little birdie told me it's someone's birthday today!"

I groaned. Celebrating by myself or with family was one thing, but having others fawn over me was low on my list of favorite things to experience.

"Change your face, Ivy," Miriam said. "That's an unbecoming look."

If I'd been ten years younger, I'd have stuck my tongue out at her.

"Happy birthday, you old thing." She hugged me quickly and then slipped a gift into my hands.

"Thank you," I said, "but you really didn't have to do this."

Boo wagged his tail and gave Miriam's knobbly knees several doggy kisses.

"At least Boo's thankful." Miriam petted him, which only doubled the ferocity of the kisses.

"I'm grateful. I just don't need a big fuss being made for my birthday, that's all." The gift was wrapped in shimmery red paper and had a huge silver bow on the front. My name had been scrawled across it in Miriam's neat, curling handwriting. The package was square and heavy. A book was my guess. More books were always welcome.

"Open it," Miriam said. "Go on."

I smiled at her as she cleared off one of the book-laden chairs beside the table and gestured for me to sit. I did so, the gift in my hands. I unwrapped it carefully, and a book fell out into my lap.

The Murder of Roger Ackroyd, by Agatha Christie.

It was a hardcover edition of my favorite book and very old, if the dog-eared cover was any indication.

"Open it," Miriam said, her voice barely containing her excitement. Boo wagged his tail and hopped back and forth, sensing her mood.

I opened it and lost my breath. It was signed by the author. The name *Agatha Christie* was written in looping letters.

"You're kidding me," I said. "Miriam? Where on earth did you get this? Last I checked, these are worth thousands of dollars. Thousands!"

"I know a guy." Miriam wriggled her eyebrows at me. "I know a guy who knows a guy, who knows a librarian who recently passed away, who had an old collection. Both guys owed me a favor."

"I can't accept this." I held it out toward her. "This is too much. You could fund a business with this kind of money."

"Then you do that," Miriam said. "If that's what you want. It's your book. I don't need the money, Ivy, you know that. I'm happy being where I am, but I get the feeling that you don't know just how appreciated you are. And I knew you wouldn't come out here to receive a gift, hence the terrified phone call."

My throat closed up.

"So, have a very happy birthday."

I blinked away tears. "I'm going to have to keep this in a glass case and never read it."

"Do what you want with it," Miriam said and gave me a hug.

I patted her on the back. "I don't know how to thank you. This is an amazing gift."

"Just have a good day," Miriam said. "I know things have been tough over the past few years, what with Darren and then your children…" Miriam had listened to me complain over the years, and I'd listened to her vent about her husband in return. Our favorite pastimes were reading, drinking coffee, and whining about life.

"I talked to Brianna today." I told her about the call and watched Miriam's expression shift from happy to irritable. "I think she's worried about the town, you know. About how safe it is. If things could just go back to the way they were when she was a girl, then she'd visit, I'm sure."

"You can't change the past, Ivy," Miriam said, ever the fount of wisdom. "Only deal with the present."

I grunted, my hands clammy on the cover of my book. I set it aside carefully, not wanting to damage it.

Boo placed his head in my lap, his expressive brown eyes peering up at me.

"What about visiting Briana and Denzel?" Miriam asked. "That's also an option, isn't it?"

"I haven't been invited."

"Maybe you should invite yourself."

It was a topic I preferred to avoid, so I rose, lifting the book off the table and hugging it to my chest. "Would you like to go to the museum tonight?" I asked. "I heard they're opening a new exhibit, and since there isn't much else to do in town, it might be fun."

"Only if we can have some pizza afterward."

"And cake," I said. "I baked one. I just forgot to bring on account of you being in mortal danger."

Miriam had the decency to blush and the audacity to give me a sneaky grin.

Overall, it wasn't a *terrible* birthday so far. Or that was what I'd thought at the time. However, the evening would soon bring events that entirely changed my perspective on the day and the week.

Four

THE SOMEWHERE MUSEUM WAS THE MOST prestigious building in town, barring the mansion-like home of the Stone family themselves. It was flanked by marble columns and possessed a grand staircase that led toward glass front doors. The hall beyond those doors was home to a ticket counter and two glass cases that held natural exhibits—lizards on one side and an arrangement of fake wolf spiders on the other.

Thankfully, the museum was pet friendly, as long as pets were kept on their leashes, so I arrived at the base of the stairs during the early hours of the evening, hoping the entry hall wouldn't be too crowded.

The only company I had outside was a homeless man wearing fingerless gloves and a penetrating stare. I dropped a few coins into his empty Styrofoam cup before moving inside.

Miriam met me ten minutes later, and we discovered the sad truth together—the museum was as empty as it always was, despite the new exhibit. The townsfolk had better places to be on a Friday night.

The only company we had outside was a homeless man wearing fingerless gloves and a penetrating stare. We dropped a few coins into his empty Styrofoam cup before moving inside.

We got our tickets and started the long tour past velvet-roped exhibitions and through halls, chatting amiably while Boo sniffed around, having the decency not to pee on anything for once.

"This must be it," Miriam said, gesturing toward a grand hall to our left. The doors were ajar, the darkness within. Words were printed on a golden plaque above the doors. ***The Rosetta Stone Star Hall.***

"Rosetta Stone Star Hall?" I asked, scratching my temple. "That's a strange choice for a name."

"Rosetta is Garret's wife," Miriam said.

"Oh, of course." I pressed a hand to my tote bag. I decided to bring my copy of the hardcover first edition Agatha Christie novel with me tonight. I didn't want to let it out of my sight. It was not only expensive but precious to me, and occasionally reaching into my bag to feel a sharp corner of the book was comforting in a way I hadn't anticipated.

Boo snuffled around at the entrance of the hall, intrigued by the darkened room beyond.

I pressed the door open, and we entered a breathtaking room. The ceiling blacked out, with a projector casting the night sky constellations onto it.

"Beautiful," Miriam cooed.

The pathway through the room was punctuated with displays that would light up at the press of a button, either playing music or a voiceover to describe interesting facts about the universe. There were exhibits about white dwarfs and how the planets were formed, ones about distant galaxies, and how early civilizations had used the night sky in their rituals and daily lives.

"This must have cost a lot," I said.

Boo whined and wagged his tail. His eyes reflected the starry projection above.

"Well, that's why it's called the Rosetta Stone Star Hall," Miriam said. "The Stones paid for all of this. It's interesting that they—"

A crash rang out, sending Boo into a frenzy of barks. I tightened my grip on the end of his leash.

A young woman stumbled past one of the exhibits,

glanced at us, then grinned and kicked over a display stand holding a glass case. The case crashed to the ground, shattering into fragments.

"Hey," I said. "What do you think you're doing?"

Boo barked and growled, jerking at the end of my leash so suddenly that it slipped out of my hand. He ran toward the woman.

"Boo, no!" I dropped my tote bag and rushed after him. It was an unfortunate fact that Boo had never gotten training, and when I'd taken him to a local dog behavioral school, they'd kicked him out after the first lesson. It was, therefore, my lot in life to chase after him and pray he didn't land himself in trouble. "Boo, heel!"

My dog skidded to a halt before the glass shards strewn across the floor.

I caught up to him and made a grab for his leash.

The woman watched with cool interest, her gaze unfocused but her smile wide. "Nice dog. I want it."

"Excuse me?"

A waft of bourbon hit my nose. She was heavily under the influence. "I want that dog. Give it to me."

"No," I said. "I'm not giving you anything except an earful."

"Who are you?" She was a starlet in a glittery red dress and high heels, wearing clothes that didn't suit the museum or the town. There were no "night clubs" in

Somewhere. The woman tossed her blonde curls over her shoulder. "I said, who are you?"

"I heard what you said. I'm choosing not to answer you," I said. "This is a brand new installation." I gestured to the hall at large. "Do you have any idea how much money it must have taken to install it?"

"Sure, I do. I'm the one who convinced Mama to install it," she said. "And since I did that, I can do whatever I want here." She strode past me, heels gritting over the broken glass, and pushed another glass case over, sending it to its doom on the hardwood floor. "And there isn't a thing you can do to stop me."

Miriam had joined us in the interim. "Cassandra Stone," she whispered to me. "Wild child. She's got a habit of causing trouble wherever she goes, and she's got more money than she knows how to spend."

The drunk woman wasn't paying attention to us anymore. Instead, she'd wandered over to one of the boxy installations at the other end of the room and was repeatedly mashing her hand down on the button so that the narrator's voice repeated over and over again.

"Reprehensible behavior," I said. "We've got to report this to the curator."

Never in my life had I witnessed such entitled behavior. Not even toddlers behaved this way.

"I don't think it will make a difference," Miriam said.

"You heard her, Ivy. Her mother's the one that paid for the whole hall, so—"

The doors creaked open, and a wispy mustache entered, followed by a hunched over man who looked as if the weight of the world was on his shoulders. The curator, Mr. Tilly. I recognized him from my previous visit.

"Oh dear," he said. "Oh no. Oh dear. Oh, not this again."

"Mr. Tilly?" I called.

He waved a hand at me. "I'm afraid the hall is closed for the evening, ladies. You'll have to leave."

"Mr. Tilly, that woman broke several glass cases," I said.

"I see that, Mrs. Jackson, but I'm afraid this is a museum issue. You need to leave," he said with an air of regret. He shuffled toward Cassandra Stone, who kept mashing her hand down on the button.

"In the beginning—" The voice was sonorous, echoing through the hall as it repeated. "In the beginning, there was—In the beginning—In the—In the beginning, there—"

"Miss Stone," Mr. Tilly called. "Miss Stone, is there anything I can help you with this evening?"

I handed Boo's leash to Miriam then and fetched my tote bag. Better to leave this to Mr. Tilly. It was my experience that aggressive people, women and men alike, usually got what was coming to them sooner or later. Miss Stone would find that out the hard way.

How right I was without knowing it at the time.

Five

An eventful evening ended with Boo and me on the sofa, nursing full bellies—mine with pizza, his with his favorite brand of dog food. I had only managed a slice of pizza where Miriam had an epic appetite and had finished the rest of it, telling me all sorts of tales about the Stone family in between bites.

The hour was late by the time I started getting ready for bed and checked my tote bag for my phone. It was at that point the realization struck home with a terrifying thump to the stomach.

The book was gone.

The first edition, hardcover Agatha Christie novel, signed by the author herself, was gone.

"No. No, no, that's not possible." I shoved what little

there was in the bag this way and that, my fingers scraping against the bottom.

The book was most definitely not there.

Boo whined at me from his doggy bed in the corner, one ear perked up, the other flopping down.

"Boo, I didn't let this bag out of my sight. There's no way it's gone." I paused, taking a breath. "Use your noggin."

And then it hit me.

I *had* let the bag out of my sight. When I had put it down in the Rosetta Stone Star Hall—still a ridiculous name—to run after Boo. The hall had been dark, and the book might have fallen out without me realizing it.

I'd been caught up in chatting to Miriam about Cassandra, the Stones, and enjoying the pizza. I hadn't bothered to dip a hand into my bag except to get my keys and unlock the cottage door when I'd arrived home.

"Boo," I said. "We have to go to the museum."

I checked the time on my phone. It was just past nine in the evening. They might not be closed yet. I'd have to convince Mr. Tilly to let me into the hall. Telling him how much the book was worth might help.

Boo hadn't budged from his puffy and well-chewed doggy bed.

I was on my own for this particular adventure. Not that I blamed him—we'd had a big and exciting day, from the mugging that morning to the strange behavior of that woman at the museum. Besides, this would be a quick walk into town. Nothing I couldn't handle on my own.

With great reluctance, I changed out of my favorite frilly nightgown and plopped my bowler hat on my head. Then I checked the pen flashlight I always kept attached to it above the rim, was in place, and then headed out.

Twenty minutes later, I arrived at the museum to find the marble columns lit with the fancy lights that bathed them a sparkling white-blue, and the glass doors closed. There was no one at the ticket counter.

"Darn it." I walked up the steps regardless, adjusting my fingers in my leather gloves—it was a cold evening, and I was grateful for my scarf and pea coat. I pressed one hand to the door, and it drifted open.

"Oh."

Open? Where was the woman who usually sat behind the ticket counter?

A wrongness drifted out from within the museum, and a feeling took hold of me. A belief that should I step across the threshold, I would find something I didn't want to. A cold shiver passed down my spine as I crossed the threshold.

"Hello?" I called out.

No one answered.

I had learned to trust my instincts when it came to

moments like these on vacation not so long ago, but I was determined not to lose that book. For heaven's sake, it was a signed Agatha Christie novel!

"Hello? Mr. Tilly? Are you in here?"

Still, no answer.

I closed the museum door before continuing down the long passage toward the Rosetta Stone Star Hall. The book would be in there, or it would be in the curator's office after someone had found it. Or it had been stolen, and I'd made this trip to have my heart broken.

The door to the hall was open a crack. I slipped inside, unclipping the pen flashlight from my bowler hat and clicking it on.

I scanned the floor and found the broken glass to the right, yet to be cleaned up, and—the book! It was right next to the exhibit where I'd dropped my bag. By some divine stroke of fate, it had fallen out of my tote bag, and no one had found it.

I collected it, triumph building in my gut, but a cold rush of foreboding came for the second time since I had entered the museum.

There was... a smell.

A metallic odor I recognized.

Blood.

I tucked the book under my arm and then turned

around, passing my flashlight beam over the exhibition, my insides churning with nerves.

A woman lay near the "Big Bang" exhibition, her hair pink. No, her hair was blonde. It was blood that had made it pink. A shard of what looked like crystal, deep sparkling blue, rested beside her. The victim wore a glittery red dress.

Cassandra Stone had been murdered, and by the looks of it, by blunt force trauma.

"Oh dear," I muttered, taking a step back. There was only one thing for it.

I exited the hall, clipped my pen flashlight back into place, then lifted my bowler hat and fetched my phone from underneath it. I dialed 911 with shaking fingers.

"AND YOU JUST WALKED IN AND SAW HER LIKE that?" Detective Darlene Darke chewed on gum while she asked me questions rather than taking notes.

"Yes," I said, ready to recount my steps for the second time. An hour had passed since I had discovered Cassandra Stone's body, and in the interim, I had been questioned twice, watched a coroner's van arrive, and witnessed police tape being erected somewhat haphazardly.

I didn't have a lot of faith in the local police—they hadn't made much of an effort to curb the rising tide of crime in Somewhere, and they were under funded. The local sheriff was located in the adjacent small town which serviced our county, so it took a lot of time to get anything done.

The local police station had one detective servicing the town—thanks to the aforementioned upswing in crime—and that was it.

"You said there was a crystal on the ground."

"A shard of crystal."

"Uh-huh. A shard." Detective Darke yawned and showed me the pink gum rolling around in her excessively moist mouth. "All right, I think that's all I need for now, Mrs. Jackson. I'll be in touch."

"That's all you need? You don't want to, I don't know, take me down to the station and interview me further?"

"Nah."

"But I found a corpse," I said.

"We've got this handled." Detective Darke flashed me an attempt at an arrogant smile. "You can run along."

"Believe me when I say I don't *run* anywhere anymore."

But the detective had already wandered off toward the museum staircase.

I could scarcely believe how lackluster her detecting skills were, but then, the town was crime-ridden. What had I expected? Then, while I was musing about how bad things had gotten, I spotted the crystal shop directly across the street. I hadn't noticed it before—as I recalled, the street that held the museum held two abandoned buildings and little else.

Except now, one of those buildings was full of the alleged murder weapon.

Six

Sleep was elusive after the discovery of Cassandra Stone's body. My short encounter with her had given me the impression that Miss Stone likely had enemies, and many of them. The family was at least partially to blame for the closure of the plastic factory.

It could be that Cassandra was the target because of her behavior in town.

Or it could be that the Stone family was the target.

A crystal as a murder weapon, though, was unique—and the murder weapon itself hadn't been recovered from the scene, only a small blue shard of crystal. That made the new crystal shop across the street even more interesting in this case.

The two pieces of evidence had to be related. What were the odds that the murder weapon hadn't come from that crystal shop? People in Somewhere weren't exactly "new age" in their beliefs.

I opened my eyes to Boo whining at the foot of my bed. His white-tipped tail wagged in and out of sight as he waited, impatiently as was his character, for me to get up.

"I'm coming." I pressed myself out of bed to discover the reason for Boo's nagging. It was well past ten in the morning. The late-night shenanigans had taken their toll.

I fed Boo his breakfast, sipped coffee, snacked on a croissant from the local bakery, and read the newspaper half-heartedly. My focus was still on the murder of Miss Stone and the likely suspects.

Mr. Tilly had a motive for murder.

That might be my intolerance showing—if I'd been faced with a spoiled rich woman trashing *my* museum, I would have lost my cool immediately.

After breakfast, I clipped on Boo's leash, escorted him out of the cottage, and started down the winding path that led past the library and into town, occasionally pressing my bowler hat to my head to keep it from blowing away.

The police line strung between the museum columns was a sobering reminder of the previous night. Mr. Tilly's car—a turquoise Chevy hatchback—was parked outside, empty. Boo and I sniffed around without breaking the rules and crossing the literal police line. We were just about to start across the street to check out the crystal shop when Mr. Tilly appeared.

From behind the police line.

"Mr. Tilly." I waved at him. Boo barked a greeting.

Mr. Tilly jolted on the spot, his wispy mustache unbrushed, making him seem even more shocked at our presence. "Mrs. Jackson." He approached, tentatively, ducking under the police line and descending the steps.

"How are you today?" I asked.

Boo took great pleasure in sniffing Mr. Tilly's front and back end, nosing his pants so that the curator had to do a sort of defensive dance, blocking Boo's nose with his hands. "I—Goodness—Just a second, I—"

"Boo." I patted my leg.

Boo gave one final, inappropriate sniff before sitting his fluffy butt down on my foot—it was his method of comforting both of us. I gathered he needed it more than me today, since I hadn't been sniffing the curator's unmentionables.

"Thank you," Mr. Tilly cleared his throat. "I've just been finishing up some work."

"In the museum?"

"Yes," Mr. Tilly said and reached up to rearrange a neat silver-gray tie. "Unfortunately, this murder business has caused a lot of trouble. You understand that Cassandra

Stone was the daughter of our greatest benefactor, Mr. Garrett Stone."

"I've heard," I said. "Have you talked to Detective Darke?"

"Oh yes. Detective Darke is an old friend, and she's gotten everything she needs from the scene, so she allowed me to enter this morning so I could continue my work."

That wasn't what I'd asked, but it was interesting information he had offered up. "I wonder how Cassandra got in," I mused. "I was so sure you would have escorted her off the premises after what happened last night."

"That was *regrettable*." Mr. Tilly smoothed his mustache, but the bristles refused to play along and stuck out again. "Miss Stone has been having, well, she *had* been having a few issues. I called her father shortly after the incident, and he came to fetch her from the hall."

"And that was the last you saw of her?" I asked.

"Yes, unfortunately. Poor girl."

Then the last person seen with Cassandra was Garrett Stone. Unless the father had seen something else—or Cassandra had sneaked out of the Stone mansion after dark.

"The strangest thing is," Mr. Tilly said, staring off into space. "I locked the museum as I usually do when I leave for the evening. I set the alarm too."

"Are you the only one that has the code?" I asked.

"There are a few others. The Stones know the code, but they don't have keys to the museum, and it's not as if there's anything that valuable in there. We're still working on getting new and interesting curios from across the state and the world." Mr. Tilly shook his head. "My only regret is that there were no cameras to catch what happened. Mr. Stone made a significant donation last week, and I was considering upping security at the museum before this happened. But with the new Rosetta Stone Star Hall launch, I was so caught up in the whirlwind of tasks that I didn't have the time."

The museum curator was decidedly itchy under the collar. He shifted his weight constantly, smoothing his mustaches.

"Are you feeling okay, Mr. Tilly?" I asked. "You seem stressed."

"Oh, you could say that," he said. "The detective might be a sweetheart, but the Stones have already called me five times this morning. Two calls from Garrett and another three from Rosetta. They're furious that the museum was left open. They're blaming me for Cassandra's... passing."

"Why?"

"The security. The lack of—" But Mr. Tilly cut off before he could get to the "good stuff." The color left his already pasty white face.

Boo let out a grumbling bark.

A police car cruised up the street and pulled to a stop outside the crystal shop opposite—my next port of call after this. Detective Darke emerged sporting a ridiculously oversized pair of aviator sunglasses like she was the star of a crime scene investigation show. She nodded at us.

"Good morning, folks," she called out. "Hope you're not up to anything illegal over there."

"Do you think if we were, we'd tell you?" I shouted back.

Mr. Tilly gave a nervous giggle before hurrying over to his hatchback, fumbling his keys out of his pocket.

Detective Darke removed her sunglasses with a flourish and sauntered over to the front of the crystal shop. The door swung open before she reached it, and the end of a shotgun barrel appeared, poking the detective in the chest.

Seven

Detective Darke fumbled for her gun, dropping her aviator sunglasses to the ground and promptly stepping on them in her frantic haste to defend herself.

"Wait," I shouted. "Detective, wait. It's not a gun."

The person holding the "shotgun" had emerged fully from the crystal shop. Her hair was puffed out in bright pink curls around her head, and she wore a long, flowing dress that dragged along the ground. Most importantly, she held a broomstick that pressed into the detective's chest. And she hadn't even noticed Detective Darke's presence yet.

She sang a tune, bobbing her head, eyes closed with what appeared to be wireless earphones in her ears. "Oh yeah!" She cried, lifting the broomstick and thumping it upward.

It struck the faded cloth awning above the door and punctured it. The singer almost-fatality struck a pose before tugging on the broom handle and realizing it wasn't coming loose. She frowned, opened her eyes, and promptly made a close acquaintance with the end of Detective Darke's gun.

During the commotion, the detective managed to get the gun out and was still processing the broomstick, the pink-haired woman, and the awful singing, which transformed into a horrified scream.

Boo added an uncertain bark to the fray.

"Please, no!" The woman raised her hands, and the broom clattered to the sidewalk. "I haven't done anything! I wasn't there, I—"

"Quiet down," Detective Darke said.

Boo and I checked both ways before crossing the street to join the pair. Or to hover nearby, safely out of shooting range.

"Lie what down?" The woman asked too loudly.

"You can lower your hands." Detective Darke started lowering her gun.

"Flower my pants?"

"I think she's got earphones in," I said helpfully.

After the third try, Detective Darke holstered her

weapon, gestured toward her ears, and motioned, plucking out earphones.

Finally, the pink-haired woman removed her earphones, and a swell of noise burst from them before she tucked them into the front pocket of her apron. "Occifer! Officer! Sorry. Hi."

Detective Darke picked up her shattered aviator sunglasses and examined them. "You owe me a pair of these," she said, gesturing with them to the woman. "You're Elsa Fraggle, correct?"

"Yes, occi—officer."

"Detective." Darke lifted the lanyard and dangled the identification card in front of Elsa Fraggle's nose.

I was, at this point, more than happy to be the silent observer. Of course, Boo had other intentions. He tugged hard on the end of his leash so that it slipped out of my hand, then ran toward Detective Darke and took a rather long sniff of her behind, his nose invading her space quite effectively.

Darke yelped and dropped her sunglasses again, and Elsa Fraggle lifted a shaking hand to her mouth to hide a smile.

"Mrs. Jackson," Darke said. "Control your animal, will you?" She fended off more of Boo's "well-intentioned" sniff attacks as I drew closer to retrieve his leash.

"He's excitable," I said. "There's a lot going on in town this morning."

"Such as?" Darke asked.

"If you're seriously asking that question, Detective, I'm alarmed." I nodded pointedly toward the museum. If Darke had finished with the scene, it should have been released, the crime scene tape removed. And if she hadn't, then why had she allowed Mr. Tilly to enter the museum?

Either way, it reeked of poor and careless police work.

"You're not suggesting that—" Darke broke off to fend off Boo's licks and sniffs.

"Are you new to town?" I asked Elsa.

The woman gave a tremble that might have passed for a nod of the head.

"You can't seriously be suggesting that the dog has any idea about the murder that took—" Another interruption as Darke spun in a circle, Boo chasing after her and barking excitedly as if it was a game.

"Do you own this shop?" Another question from Darke for the pink-haired Elsa.

"Yeah," she squeaked.

"Welcome to Somewhere," I said. "It's better than nowhere and worse than most places."

"That's—" Darke cut off, trying to shoo Boo. "Would you call your dog back? I'm trying to interview a suspect here."

"A suspect!" Elsa stumbled back a step, tripped over the fallen broomstick, and landed on her bottom. "Suspected of what?"

"Murder," I said. "Cassandra Stone was murdered last night. By a crystal."

"Would you kindly, just—" Darke flapped her hands at Boo, and he tried licking them.

I saved her from Boo's attention by bringing him back to my side and taking a firm grip on the end of his leash. That was more than enough torture for one day. Even if Darke did deserve it after her shoddy police work.

I'd encountered the detective once before—when I'd reported my car stolen six months ago. She'd done nothing but express sympathies and went shopping for sunglasses, apparently. The car had never been recovered, and I was stuck hoofing it everywhere. Good for the digestive system but terrible for my temperament.

"Mrs. Fraggle," Detective Darke said.

"It's Miss Fraggle," she whispered.

"*Miss* Fraggle," Detective Darke said. "Let's take a walk together. I've got some questions for you."

"A walk?" Fraggle asked. "But—"

"We need to talk away from prying ears."

"Ears can't pry, Detective," I said.

"If they could, I'm sure yours would be experts at it." Touche.

"I'm not here for any reason other than to walk my dog," I said. "It's lovely to meet you, Elsa."

Elsa gave me a shy smile.

I wasn't known for being particularly welcoming around town. Then again, I wasn't known very well since I'd kept to myself since Darren's passing. This was a great opportunity to change that and find out more about Fraggle in one fell swoop.

"This way, please." Detective Darke herded her away from the crystal shop, having the basic decency to allow her to lock up the front door first. Boo barked goodbye as the pair walked off, and I let out a breath.

This was unorthodox. The second strange thing that the detective had done in a short time—she hadn't correctly secured the crime scene and hadn't interviewed the suspect in an interrogation room.

Was she that lazy?

I collected Boo's leash and started the walk home, determined to find out more about the victim, the Stone family, and this new entity—Elsa Fraggle.

Eight

My primary confidante arrived at noon that day to discuss the coming of spring flowers and how big the Stone funeral would be. The two topics were technically related, albeit macabre—but I enjoyed the macabre. I'd always had a fascination with murder mysteries, horror movies, and a glass of red wine. The glass of red wine was out of the question given the hour, no matter how much Miriam protested that it was "five o'clock somewhere".

Boo was satisfied with himself after his morning "adventures" but not enough to keep from romancing the chihuahua next door, trying to appeal to her through the fence separating my cottage from the unfriendly neighbors'.

"What is he up to out there?" Miriam had a mug sandwiched between her palms, her head tilted as she watched

Boo out by the fence. "Does he normally rub his behind against the slats like that?"

"Yes."

"You might want to get him checked for worms."

"I have, multiple times," I said. "It's not worms he's after, but a chihuahua that's equal parts cute and annoying," I said.

This was one of the first times I'd had anyone in my home since Darren's death, but after a recent cruise to the Bahamas—a failed cruise to be precise—I'd promised myself I would face my problems. One of them was my "grumpy" image in Somewhere.

"Would you like a piece of cake?" I asked.

"That would be great." Miriam drifted away from the windows and took a seat at my square kitchen table. It was one that Darren had chosen for us after I'd insisted that the old table—big enough for our children and their grandkids—was too large for the cottage. We'd moved out of our old house years ago.

Miriam accepted her slice of cake and tucked in. "This is delicious, Ivy. You've got a natural talent for baking."

"I just followed a recipe." I smiled at her.

Miriam had invited me over to the library and her home plenty of times in the past few years, and we'd created a friendship that had blossomed over time without me realizing it. A warm and unfamiliar feeling settled in my chest. Perhaps, it was the sound of another person's voice in my cottage apart from my own that was bringing it on.

Our conversation drifted naturally from the library to the museum and then to the shocking news of the day.

"Everyone's talking about it," Miriam said. "The local newspaper is going to run a weekly feature until it's solved. Or they were—we'll see what the Stones have to say about that."

"The Stones seem to have a lot more control over Somewhere than I gave them credit for."

"That's because you've had your head buried in the sand for the past couple of years," Miriam said matter-of-factly. That was fine. I preferred people who said things as they were rather than dancing around a subject. "You're our very own grumpy ostrich."

There was that word again. Darn it. I could almost hear Darren chuckling at me from above. "My head couldn't have been that deep. What else have I missed? Let me guess, that Stones have another daughter named Sapphire, and they own the local mortuary."

"No, but they do have one named Garnet who moved out of town a couple of years ago. And they own plenty of real estate. An unfortunate amount," Miriam said.

I took a bite of cake and chewed slowly. "They could have done it."

"Done what?" Miriam gave me a scandalized look. "You can't seriously mean that the Stones killed their own daughter."

"People have done worse and stranger things."

"According to the police, they're clear," Miriam said. "Oh, don't look at me like that. The library is practically a gossip highway. People come to trade stories, whether they're in paperback format or verbal."

"I believe they call that an audiobook."

Miriam laughed, but then her expression grew serious once again. "The point is, I've heard some interesting things."

"Care to share them?"

"You saw how Cassandra behaved on the night at the museum?"

"With my own two eyes. Reading glasses excluded."

"That isn't the first time she's done something like that. She's whipped people into a frenzy time and time again. She loves... *loved* making people angry because she knew they couldn't do anything about it. The entire town, all the people who have power at least, is in the Stones' pocket."

"She was destructive. No offense, but that's not a revelation."

Miriam gestured with a piece of cake on the end of her

dessert fork. "I'm getting there. Apparently, she was seen arguing with a friend the day before the murder."

"A friend?" Could Elsa Fraggle have been friends with that beast of a woman? I didn't make a habit of disrespecting the dead, but the young lady had barely qualified for the phrase "lady."

"She's just gotten back to town. Joanie Parker. Astronomer."

"She's an astronomer? Here?"

"That's what I thought too, but it's the truth," Miriam said. "She studied astrophysics at the University of Ohio, so I'd wager she has a bright future ahead of her."

"That would give her a lot to lose," I said. "Do you know what they were arguing about?"

Miriam set down her fork and leaned back in my creaking kitchen chair, her arms folded across the neat sweater vest she'd chosen for another cold spring day. "Not sure, but it might have had something to do with the museum. Or not. I really don't know. But people are talking about it."

"Joanie Parker," I said, making a mental note of it.

"I'm not sure where she's staying at the moment, but the rumor is that she had asked to live with the Stones."

"The two women were that close?"

"Old high school friends," Miriam said. "And if she's

living there, it's no wonder we don't see her around town much. The Stones are infamously private. Probably because most of the people in Somewhere hate their guts for what they did to the town. Selling the darn plastics factory to those shysters who closed the place and tanked the town's economy. It's not like Somewhere's going to do a roaring trade in tourism, no matter how many museums the Stones fund. The place is in a state of disrepair. Crime is rampant."

I nodded.

"People in town are talking about the murder because it was Cassandra Stone who was killed, and because it was done in such a... different way. But people aren't shocked. Because they're getting used to the crime levels. You know how it is, Ivy. Abandoned homes. People moving out, and no one moving in to replace them. Somewhere property is a bad investment, as bad as they come, and the worse that gets, the poorer people get, the higher the crime rates."

I patted her on the arm. Miriam had lived in Somewhere as long as I had—that was to say, she was born and raised here. It hurt to see the town spiral, especially when it meant the family wouldn't come to visit because of it.

"If things could just go back to the way they were—"

"Not the way they were, Ivy. To something better. There's no going back now."

Boo's barking drove me from the table to the window. He had managed to summon the chihuahua to the fence, and the pair were trying to lick each other through the slats.

"I'd better go," Miriam said. "I have a shift at the library this afternoon. Did you finish that James Patterson novel you borrowed?"

"Almost."

"Well, drop by anyway."

"I will. I need to go into town for some essentials, anyway."

Essentially, I wanted to snoop.

Nine

Our first stop was at the grocery store to grab some dog food for Boo and a few of those microwaveable meals for me. When I could help it, I avoided cooking nowadays—it only reminded me of cooking for a family of four, and I wasn't used to portioning down to one. Besides, roasting chickens and eating well were reserved for the precious occasions I got to spend with my children.

Unfortunately, the grocery shopping and the surly teenage cashier who rang up my goods and pretended like I didn't exist were the least of my problems. The book store down the road was a constant temptation, even though the books in its windows were faded from being displayed in the same formation in the window for too long.

I paused outside it, considering the titles, while Boo ran in circles around my legs, tying me up with his leash.

"You're not going to achieve anything good by doing that," I said to him. "If I trip and break my hip, who's going to feed you?"

Boo ran the other way, untying me from the mess. No one could convince me that animals didn't understand what we were saying at this point.

The book store was a short walk from the museum and the crystal shop across, so we took a turn in that direction, pushing the shopping-cart/wheeled walker combination I'd bought online. Internet shopping had some benefits, even if it meant obsessively checking how long my order would take to reach me.

I tied Boo's leash around the handle of my wheeled walker as we approached Artifact Street—how much had the Stones paid to have that street name changed?

The museum was closed, the glass doors restricted by an official police seal and the lights off inside. Regrettably, the crystal shop was as dark as the abandoned building beside it.

"Do you want to go to the park, Boo?" He could play while I rested my feet and pondered the case.

Boo barked in the affirmative, and we took the short road past the museum to the park just behind it. The grass was long, and one of the swings hung skew on its chain, moving eerily as if someone had just gotten off it.

I took a seat on the park bench and let Boo roam free.

A small pile of cardboard and clothing rested against the fence nearby, and I frowned at it, unsure of what it was or where it had come from. I rooted around in my tote bag for my book.

A strong scent of cheap perfume invaded my nostrils, ruining the gentle scent of the grass and the spring breeze.

"What you got there?" A feminine voice spoke in my ear.

I turned my head and came face-to-face with a middle-aged, gold-toothed behemoth of a woman. She wouldn't have been out of place in a wrestling ring, but she wore a long trench coat, the ends of which had dragged through the dirt one too many times.

"Who are you?" I asked.

"Mind if I join you?" She plopped down beside me before I answered.

Boo hadn't noticed her yet. He was too busy sniffing the bottom of the suspended trash can near the playground.

"Who are you?" I repeated.

"You don't know?" She gave me another of those broad smiles, showing off that she had more than one gold tooth. "Shoot, I thought everybody in town knew who I was by now." There was a mean set to her jaw and a wickedness in her eyes.

"Question your logic," I said evenly, placing my tote

bag to one side. "If I knew who you were, would I have asked?"

"Not unless you wanted to annoy me." She sat back with a huffing self-satisfied sigh. "And not many people would dare do that. Queenie."

"That's an interesting name." I checked what Boo was up to, dividing my attention equally between him and the newcomer.

"It's a nickname. Shortened for my title."

I didn't ask.

She leaned forward, balancing her forearms on her thighs and considering me. "This is my park," she said.

"You own the park?"

It wasn't a serious question. The park belonged to Somewhere and to its people.

"Sure do," she said. "Do you know what's down there?" She gestured vaguely past the park in the opposite direction to the museum.

"Young woman," I said. "I've lived here longer than you've drawn breath. It's safe to say I know where everything is situated in my home town."

"That so?" She arched an eyebrow that was drawn onto her tan skin. "I've never seen you around here before."

"Then you haven't been paying much attention," I said.

Queenie froze and then forced out a laugh. "Let me fill in the blanks for you, *old* woman. This is my park. Just down that-away are the train tracks, and beyond that is my part of town. Sewerville."

There wasn't a place in Somewhere called Sewerville. There was one called Sweetville, however, and it was the area closest to the old abandoned plastics factory. A lot of the folks who had worked in the factory lived there, and it was, unfortunately, a poor area that needed an injection of care and cash. Neither was coming any time soon.

"See, that's why they call me Queenie," the arrogant would-be wrestler continued, pressing a massive hand to her chest. "Because I am the Queen of Sewerville. The Queen of Rats, they like to call me, and this park is my territory."

I tucked my tongue behind my teeth and gave a shrill whistle. Boo came running and stopped beside the walker, crouching low, his teeth bared and a growl in his throat.

Queenie watched him with an air of a predator sizing up an opponent.

"Unless you've been appointed the queen of the universe," I said. "Or even the queen of the town, for that matter, then you don't own this park. It's public property. Not that it matters who owns it. Kindly leave me alone."

Queenie snorted deeply and spat off to one side.

"Anyone who uses my park has to pay a toll. So, what do you got in those brown paper bags?"

"Nothing for you."

Boo growled deeper.

"I wouldn't get on my bad side if I were you, lady." Queenie rose from her seat and towered over me. "You don't know who you're messing with."

I got up, albeit with a few aches and pains I refused to show in my expression, and stared her down. "I don't care who you think you are. I won't pay a toll for using a public park, and you'd better leave me alone before I report you to the police."

Queenie guffawed. "I like your backbone," she said. "Be a shame if it got broken. See, the police don't care about this town any more than you or I do. They won't stop me from doing what *I want*." The last two words came out hissed.

"There's were you're wrong," I said. "I care about this town. And it's people like you who are driving it into the ground." I gave a second sharp whistle, and Boo launched himself toward Queenie.

She let out a grunt and darted around the park bench. Boo made to follow her, but I stopped him with another whistle.

He might not be a traditionally trained dog, but it was in moments like these that I was grateful for—

Boo forgot about the previous command and darted around the park bench, snapping at Queenie's heels. She gave me a look of pure rage before racing off across the park. Boo chased her right to the end before returning, a bounce in his step.

"Proud of yourself?"

He howl-talked back at me.

"You should be," I said and petted him. "Good boy. Now, let's get home."

Ten

OUR RETURN HOME WAS DELAYED WHEN WE rounded the corner, entering Artifact Street, to find Mr. Tilly's car parked outside the museum again. A full-blown argument was underway in front of the doors.

Mr. Tilly and his wispy mustache had been cornered by an attractive young brunette with tan legs and fire in her tone. Mr. Tilly preferred to avoid women, and people in general, when he got the opportunity, but this was one of those times when opportunity and fate strongly disagreed.

Boo and I stopped at the base of the grand museum steps to listen in on the conversation.

"What do you mean it's closed?" The fire-eyed woman had both fists on her hips. "It can't be closed. You agreed to meet with me today, and I'm here, on time. This is unfair. It's—"

"Miss Parker, I understand this is very upsetting for you, but things in Somewhere run at a slower pace than they do in the big cities."

This was Joanie Parker, the astronomer and alleged friend of the deceased. If my ears could have pricked up like Boo's, they would have.

"Things don't run slower here," Joanie said. "I'm from here. You're just being a slippery eel."

Those were strong words.

Mr. Tilly's gray eyelashes fluttered at the accusation. "A slippery—How dare you! I'm the curator of this establishment. Insulting me is the last thing you should do." Mr. Tilly was so involved in the conversation he hadn't noticed Boo and me standing at the base of the stairs yet. His expression was sour as lemons as his gaze swept over Joanie.

"I'm telling you, I'll discuss this with... I don't know. The mayor. Or I'll go to the newspaper. I know that you're denying me the job for a reason."

"I have no idea what you're talking about," Mr. Tilly said.

"There's no good reason for you *not* to hire me. I'm overqualified. You just opened an entire exhibition that could have been improved if I had been a part of your team. It's not like you don't have the money since you're sponsored by the richest family in town. So, someone's telling you what to do."

"Regardless of that, do you really think cornering me is going to get you the job?"

"I don't know what else to do, Mr. Tilly," Joanie said. "I studied for years, and there are no other jobs in this town. There aren't even that many jobs in the city. Times are tough for everyone. If you send me away, you—"

"Your behavior has been inappropriate for weeks now. What makes you think I'd want you as a part of my staff?" Mr. Tilly countered.

The curator's back was pressed right up against that official police seal. I kept Boo at my side and still—or as still as I could—while I listened. When the pair moved, I'd hopefully catch a glimpse of the door. If Mr. Tilly had broken the seal, well, now...

"Name one time my behavior has been inappropriate," Joanie said, raising a finger. "Apart from now."

"You think I didn't see you snooping around in the Rosetta Stone Star Hall last night?"

Joanie grumbled, and I caught the tail-end of her words. "—dumb name."

"You're walking yourself toward a ban from the museum in general."

"I was attending the event like any other member of

the town," Joanie said. "By the way, several of your scripts for the voiceovers were inaccurate. You could have avoided that if you had just hired me when you were supposed to."

"I'm not supposed to hire anyone!" Mr. Tilly snapped. "Now get out of my way, you petulant girl." He pushed past her and started down the steps, finally spotting Boo and me there.

"Afternoon, Mr. Tilly," I said, leaning on my walker. "Everything all right?"

"Everything is perfectly fine, thank you." He strode toward his car and got into it.

Before he could shut the door, Joanie darted down the steps and caught the handle. She wrenched it open and glared at him. "I've worked too long and too hard not to get what I want," she said. "You won't stop me, Tilly. If I have to go to the papers, I will. If I have to talk to the mayor, I will. And if it's Garrett Stone, I have to convince..."

Mr. Tilly paled. "You're making a scene," he mumbled.

Boo barked, rising onto all fours.

"That's the thing, Tilly," Joanie said. "I'll make a scene if I have to. I'm desperate. What don't you get?"

Mr. Tilly managed to wrest the door free of her grip and slam it shut. He pressed the lock down, peering out at her as if he'd seen a ghost. He started the Chevy's engine and drove off at high speed, skidding around the corner and disappearing from sight.

Joanie stood exactly where he'd left her on the sidewalk, her hands balled into fists and tears in her angry, blue eyes.

I had the sense to check whether the police seal on the door was broken—it wasn't—before turning my attention back to Joanie. She was frozen in that spot, staring at the crystal shop across the road, or the abandoned building, or just space and time itself.

I cleared my throat. "Miss Parker?"

Joanie shook her head rapidly as if to clear it, then turned to me. "Do I know you?"

"No. My name is Ivy Jackson. You look shaken up."

"It's been a tough few days," she said. "That idiot…"

"Mr. Tilly?"

"Yeah."

She was young, possibly in her late twenties, well-educated, and pretty. If she couldn't find a job, then it was no wonder Somewhere was in so much trouble. "You'll get back on the wagon," I said in an attempt to be kind.

"Wagon? What wagon?"

"It's a saying," I said. "You're looking for a job at the museum?"

Joanie exhaled through her teeth, visibly relaxing as we talked. Her gaze traveled to Boo, and a smile parted her lips briefly. Boo had that effect on people. It was difficult to be mad when a handsome border collie gave you puppy dog eyes.

"I'm an astronomer," she said. "Technically, I studied astrophysics."

"And you came back to town to find work?"

"Not really," she said. "My parents used to live here, but they moved a few years back when the crime started getting out of hand."

I nodded. "I can understand that."

"Wait." She clicked her fingers and pointed at me. "You're... Aren't you Mr. Jackson's wife? Darren Jackson?"

"That's right," I said, a flutter starting in my chest at the mention of my husband's name. "He passed away just over a year ago."

"Oh, I'm sorry," she said.

"Thank you." I hesitated. "Would you like to come over to my house for coffee and cake?" It was one thing to be hospitable. It was another to take advantage of the present situation. Mr. Tilly had mentioned she'd been at the museum last night.

A suspect? A witness?

"That would be lovely," Joanie said. "Thank you."

I grinned. "Right this way, my dear."

Eleven

Two guests in my home in the span of a day? Darren had to be in shock and awe at my bravery. Or foolishness. He would know since he had a better view of the issues down here. I hoped he would guide me in any way he could, whether a gentle nudge, a small sign, or a blaring car horn waking me in a cold sweat. The latter was a prank he'd played on me when we'd been in the honeymoon phase of our relationship.

"Mrs. Jackson?"

"Sorry, dear," I said, moving the coffee pot toward the tray where two mugs waited. "I was lost in thought."

"No problem." Joanie brushed her hands off on her faded blue jeans and helped me carry the tray over to the coffee table in the living area portion of the kitchen-living room combo. I had placed cakes, coffees, sugar, and cream on the tray.

Joanie took her coffee black and avoided the cake, possibly because she was watching her weight. She was so slim I could believe it.

Boo lay in front of the door, his head resting on his paws, drifting in and out of sleep. The Finks, my neighbors, had left a rude note taped to my door threatening to report me for disturbing the peace after Boo and their chihuahua had licked each other senseless through the fence.

It was an empty threat. I was more concerned about what the licking would do to the wood over time. The last thing I needed was a conjoined front yard with the Finks.

"How long have you been back in town?" I lifted a cup to my lips, inhaling and relishing the aroma. Darren had despised coffee—always made him run for the bathroom.

"Just a few months," Joanie said. "I've been staying with the Stones."

"Oh? You're well-connected. As I understand it, the Stones are well-off."

She didn't need to know that I was acutely familiar with the Stones and their "work."

"They're rich." Joanie shrugged. "Not that it means anything for me. I'm just lucky that poor Cassandra managed to convince her parents to let me stay with them."

"Poor Cassandra?" I gasped. "Of course. The woman who was..."

"Yeah," Joanie said, moving her hand over one arm. She drew it away again, and I noticed two long scratch marks against her tan skin. "It happened last night during the museum's opening of the new exhibition."

"I'm glad I didn't see anything," I said.

"Me neither," Joanie replied.

"You were there too?" Joanie likely didn't know how much of her conversation I'd overheard with Mr. Tilly. That gave me the brief upper hand in this conversation.

"I was there," she said. "Briefly. I wanted to see what the museum had set up in the hall. You know, I care about my work, and I figured that if they'd done a good job, they wouldn't need me. But they did a terrible job." She clicked her tongue. "Anyway, I left before anything happened to Cassandra." She took a sip of coffee and then patted underneath either of her eyes, cleaning away her tears. Allegedly.

"We visited later in the evening," I said. "What time were you there?"

"Oh, before seven." Joanie set down her cup, and coffee sloshed over the edge and onto my silver tray. "I didn't want to hang around in case Mr. Tilly got annoyed. Turns out he got annoyed, anyway."

"My condolences."

"For Mr. Tilly's anger?" Joanie laughed, then flapped a hand, growing serious. "I know. For Cassandra. Thank you. We were close in high school, but we kinda drifted apart after I left for university."

"Oh."

"Yeah, we argued a lot when I came back between semesters before my parents moved. I think she was a little jealous that I was doing stuff with my life while she was stuck here." A wistful look came over Joanie. "Cassandra was made for bigger and better things than this town. She wanted to be a supermodel or an actress or any number of famous careers. It's a pity she'll never be able to achieve any of that."

"And you preferred the stars?"

"I've been obsessed with astrophysics since I was a girl. Cassandra and I would sneak out at night together. She would text boys, and I would lie on my back, staring up at the stars and considering the possibilities."

A comfortable quiet drifted between us, and I allowed it to stay for a while and lull my guest into a sense of ease.

"I wonder who did it," I said.

Joanie shivered, shaking her head. "I don't know. I

think, now, this is nothing against Cassandra, but she had a lot of enemies."

"Enemies, eh?"

"Yeah. Cassandra had a natural aptitude for living large and getting under people's skin. I know for a fact she's gotten into trouble with the cops a couple of times. And many people in town wouldn't have minded if she was out of the way." Joanie rolled her eyes to the left and downward as if she didn't want to say but couldn't resist gossiping. "One of those people happened to be right across the road from the museum that night."

"Are you talking about the owner of the crystal shop?"

"How did you know?"

"I saw the police talking to her this morning," I said.

"Oh yeah?" Joanie perked up. "That makes sense. Elsa and Cassandra *did not* get along. Cassandra called her a pink-haired weirdo, and Elsa called Cassandra a materialistic capitalistic cog in the machine of a broken society."

One of those insults was superior to the other.

"Both were right," Joanie laughed, but it cut off, and that unhappy expression returned to her features again. "And now that I think about it..."

I waited, my coffee cooling rapidly in my hands.

"Now that I think about it, I'm sure I saw the lights on in the crystal shop when I left the museum last night." Joanie brushed her palms over her jeans. "And I know that

Elsa doesn't live in the crystal shop. She has a house in Sweetsville. So what was she doing there that late? Unless she was cleaning or something."

"Interesting."

"Yeah. And kind of scary," Joanie said. "I just can't believe there's a murderer in our midst. And that they did it in such a vicious way."

We finished our coffee, tending toward regular small talk—of which I was *not* a fan—and Joanie rose after another ten minutes of chatting, thanking me profusely for my hospitality. She used my bathroom and then left, giving Boo a quick pat on the head.

"It sounds to me like we've got to pay a certain crystal shop owner a visit," I said. "Tomorrow. I've had enough of walking and arguing with strangers for one day."

Boo barked to be let outdoors, and I took great pleasure in releasing him on the fence and the chihuahua.

Twelve

BOO AND I WERE FREE TO ROAM SOMEWHERE TO our heart's content, and the truth was, our neighbors, the Finks, probably preferred it when we weren't home. They certainly enjoyed the reprieve from Boo's insistent fence-licking.

But after the murder, lack of sleep, and a full day of talking to suspects and that ominous woman in the park, we were utterly pooped.

It was only the next day when we had the energy to take our leave of the cottage once more and head toward the crystal shop.

I was, by this point, determined to get my hands on the jumpy, broomstick-wielding crystal shop owner. She was part of the key to this mystery, whether she was the actual murderer or not. The innocent singing could all be an act. What better way to hide in plain sight than to act hapless?

Or she was a hapless woman—either way, worth the investigation, if only to help her overcome her haplessness in relation to the case.

Detective Darke might be out of her depth with the case, but connecting the murder weapon to the owner of the store that was stocked full of them was within her mental reach.

Boo padded along the sidewalk, swishing his tail happily as was his way and occasionally stopping to sniff wet patches, suspicious trash cans, or blades of grass that shouldn't have caused him alarm.

I pressed my bowler hat to my head and kept a weather eye on the horizon, just in case this "Queen of Rats" decided to make a reappearance. Something told me she wouldn't be as easily deterred the second time around.

We entered Artifact Street, chased by the bright morning sunlight, and found it mostly empty. The seal was intact on the museum doors, a small Christmas miracle at this point—call it Christmas in May—and the crystal shop doors were open. A second miracle.

I rapped once on the open glass door, noting the hole in the cloth awning hadn't yet been repaired, and Boo barked to announce our presence.

A shout of alarm came from inside, and Elsa Fraggle

appeared, looking as frazzled as she had the last time we'd seen her.

"Oh, hello," she said. "It's you. The lady from yesterday."

"Ivy Jackson. This is Boo."

Elsa stuck out her hand, and I took it. "Lovely to meet you both." She bent and put out a hand to Boo. He gave her his paw—there had to be an angel watching over us today with this many miracles—and they shook too.

"Come inside," she said, then hesitated. "You don't have anything against crystals, do you?"

"Against crystals?"

She made a small noise of ascent in her throat.

"Why would we have anything against crystals?" We entered the shop, and the confusing scents of lavender, sage, and... what I could only describe as "old things" filled my nostrils. Boo sneezed twice, shaking his head afterward.

"A lot of people in Somewhere seem to have a problem with them," she said. "They think I'm some kind of, oh, I don't know, like some new age spiritual person or whatever. They all think I believe that crystals have all sorts of properties when really, I just like how they look. Not that I have any problem with people who do believe in that kind of thing. I don't anyway, but the townsfolk definitely do. Definitely. I just make jewelry. That's all. Just jewelry."

Apparently, Elsa had been waiting a while to get all of that out. Boo and I stared at her, both overwhelmed by the diatribe and expecting more.

We weren't wrong.

"Can you believe that?" Elsa continued, sweeping into her shop, where rows of crystals were on shelves, either large stones or collections of smaller ones in various shapes and sizes. A wall behind the counter held finished jewelry—sparkling and beautiful jewelry—tiaras, rings, necklaces, and bracelets.

I opened my mouth to compliment her on the creations, but she was already on to the next portion of her tirade.

"I keep trying to advertise it around town. I've put out, like, flyers and posters and all sorts of things stating that the crystal shop is for jewelry. I figured I'd kill two birds with one stone—see it's free advertising if the people do decide to visit, and on the other, it's educating people about the shop and how I'm not some evil witch who's casting a spell on everyone, or trying to murder people with crystals, or—" Elsa ran out of breath at last. She sucked in another one. "But it doesn't seem to be working. Even that detective that came around yesterday thinks I had something to do with what happened at the museum. Did you hear about that?"

"Yes, we—"

"Just my luck that Cassandra Stone, of all people, would go and get herself murdered," she grunted. "And with a stone. A stone! It's terrible, but it's also not a shock after everything she put me through and put other people through and..." She trailed off and shook her head, rounding the counter and leaning atop it. "All I'm trying to do is, like, get my shop up and running. I never thought I'd wind up in a town like Somewhere."

"What brings you here?" I squeezed in.

The only solace in being overwhelmed by her words was the thought that Detective Darke had experienced similar. Or worse.

"Where? To Somewhere? I wanted to move away from the big city after my apartment was broken into, but it turns out this place isn't that much safer than the city. People getting murdered left and right, crazed, angry townsfolk trying to break into my shop or attacking me, verbally for now, in the street because, like, I'm the woo-woo crystal lady who runs the shop, so I have to be evil. It's like a Salem witch-hunt without the witches."

If only Boo would distract her for just a second so I could ask a question. But I was hardly that passive of a woman.

Elsa opened her mouth to continue the tirade, and I tapped my hand down on the countertop, silencing her with the gesture and a quick smile.

"Did you know Cassandra Stone?"

"Yes. Unfortunately. The woman detested me because of all the reasons I just listed. That or she just wanted to make my life miserable because she could."

"And you're aware that she was murdered by blunt force trauma. By a crystal."

Elsa gave a doleful nod, if a nod could be doleful.

"And as far as I know, your crystal shop is the only one in town."

Another nod, even more, unhappy than the first. Suddenly, Elsa had lost her voice.

"What do you think about that?"

"My shop was broken into," Elsa said. "Two days before the murder. I thought it was vandalism like the last couple of times, people have been throwing rocks through the door and all of that, but when I took stock the other day, I noticed that one of my most rare crystals was missing. A sapphire."

"An actual sapphire?"

"Yes. A big one. It was worth a lot of money, too," Elsa said. "I'm not great at keeping track of these types of things, so it was quite a shock when I saw it was missing."

There had been blue shards on the floor next to Cassandra's corpse. The murderer must have hit her incredibly hard to have shattered the sapphire.

But why use it as a murder weapon? It seemed like a heck of a lot of effort to go through.

I was milliseconds from asking her when the door to the crystal shop slapped open, and a reed-thin woman draped in pearls and cashmere stormed into the shop.

Thirteen

I HADN'T REALIZED THAT THE DOOR HAD SWUNG closed as we'd been talking, but it was probably better that way. The cream cardigan, who had barged in looked as if she liked to make an entrance. Objective achieved in this case.

Boo started barking like a man possessed while I took the moment of chaos and distraction to consider the newcomer in all her wealth and apparent glory.

The blonde hair was perfectly coiffed, and the perfume was expensive and overrode the scents of sage and dust. The expression was one of dignified horror that the rich wore well and the poor shied away from.

"You... You..." The newcomer waved her hands around.

I had seen her in passing around town, and though I

was now a hermit, that hadn't always been the case. This was Rosetta Stone, or Rose, as I'd always known her back before Darren had passed and when I'd been more in touch with the world.

Elsa Fraggle shrank in on herself and looked ready to put up a cross to ward off evil. That was duly ironic in this case, given that Elsa was the one who was considered Maleficent by Somewherians.

"Mrs. Stone," she squeaked out. "Hello, Mrs. Stone. How are you today?"

"How am I? How. Am. I?" Mrs. Stone huffed and puffed like she'd never heard anything as insulting during her entire existence. "How do you think I am?" The words were thunderously loud in the small shop. "After everything you've done."

"Everything I've done?" Elsa trembled. "I'm not sure what you mean. I haven't—"

Mrs. Stone approached like a predator cornering its prey, heels clicking on the wooden flooring in the crystal shop. "First, you move to this town and open this abomination of a shop. And then, you have the audacity to deny that it's an abomination."

"I'm just trying to sell jewelry," Elsa cried.

I kept a firm grip on the end of Boo's leash in case he decided to try anything untoward. He didn't like people who talked in aggressive tones. Boo firmly believed that only he was allowed to have a loud bark, and that was only because he didn't have much of a bite unless someone was in danger.

A moral ethos to live by.

"Sell your evil, curse witch jewelry," Mrs. Stone snapped, spittle flying from her lips. "And I wasn't finished talking."

"But—"

"You will speak when I'm done!" she snapped.

Boo gave a warning bark, but Mrs. Stone ignored him.

"You have desecrated the sanctity of our town, and now, you have desecrated my family."

"I didn't do anything," Elsa whispered, almost mouthing it under the onslaught from Mrs. Stone.

"You murdered my daughter!"

"I didn't. I would never!"

"I don't have time for your lies," Mrs. Stone growled, and Boo mimicked her. "I came to warn you that your time in this town is almost up."

"W-What?"

"You're not going to get away with this for much longer. I've talked directly to the sheriff about your inter-ference here, and he agrees with me. You are the most likely suspect!" She pointed at Elsa with a flourish.

I liked to think I was a fairly religious woman, but I wasn't about to partake in a crusade against a woman who was just trying to live her life. Tolerance was a value that was sadly lacking in modern society—unless it was tolerance for murderers. There was a lack of balance in Somewhere and the world in general. People were demonized for how they lived their lives, while others were given slaps on the wrist for committing serious crimes.

All in all, Rosetta Stone had started to remind me of the preacher from "Footloose" and who could forget how that movie had turned out?

"I didn't do anything wrong." Tears spilled down Elsa's cheeks.

Now, she may well have been the murderer, and she was a suspect as the woman who owned what was effectively the "murder weapon shop," but that was what a court of law was for.

Due process.

There was no need for a court of public opinion.

Rosetta Stone drew herself up, tugging furiously on her pearl necklace, so much so that I was shocked it didn't break. "Lie all you want, young woman, but you won't get away with this. You won't taint the future of our town with your disrespect any longer. You—"

I cleared my throat softly.

Mrs. Stone swept her imperious gaze in my direction.

I pulled on the tip of my bowler hat in greeting. "Mrs. Stone. Allow me to interrupt your tirade," I said.

"I don't see why I should allow you to do any—"

"Correct me if I'm wrong, but aren't you married to Garrett Stone?"

"What's that got to do with anything?" Rosetta asked, pressing a finger to the end of her sharp nose, smearing the contouring makeup there.

"Mr. Stone used to own the plastic factory, isn't that correct?" I asked.

"We co-owned it," she said, a hint of pride entering her tone.

"Then you don't really have a leg to stand on when it comes to lecturing people about 'ruining' this town, do you?"

"What on earth do you—?"

"You two sold that plastics factory to the same shyster who ran it into the ground," I said evenly. "If not for you, the town wouldn't be so run down, and it wouldn't be this crime-ridden. But then, that's what you wanted all along, isn't it? To rule in chaos and have complete control over the outcome of every decision in Somewhere."

Mrs. Stone's mouth dropped open, flapping like a flag in the wind.

"I suggest you leave this woman alone and allow the police to investigate the murder without interference. As the courts intended it."

Mrs. Stone glared at me, hatred brewing in her eyes. "And who, might I ask, are you?"

"Ivy Jackson," I said, flicking up my bowler hat ever so slightly. Boo barked to back me up, then sat down on my foot. "And this is Boo. We're here to clean up this town." I kept a firm grip on the end of Boo's leash and took a step toward the woman. "Even if that means confronting bullies like you, Mrs. Stone."

Rosetta made a noiseless gasp.

A silence permeated the dusty interior of the crystal shop. Boo held himself dead still, staring down our common enemy, ready to move at a moment's notice or the smallest impetus from me.

"I-I'm afraid I'm going to have to ask you both to leave," Elsa said, warbling the words out. "It's almost time for my mid-morning jewelry crafting seminar. P-Please leave."

Rosetta cast a glance in her direction before lifting two fingers and poking them in my direction, a signal that she was doubtless "watching me." Or it was a new-fangled method for warding off evil. Who knew?

Boo and I waited for her to head out before leaving ourselves. I was in the mood for a morning nap after the shenanigans, and Boo was in need of a session of fence-licking.

Fourteen

I had just about finished my James Patterson novel by noon and had put on a pot of coffee when a knock rattled against my front door. Boo, who had opted for a midday snooze in his doggy bed, released a muted bark of protest at the interruption. I was equally perplexed.

Yes, I'd invited Miriam over and had Joanie for coffee, but surely people weren't actively seeking me out. I was still that "grumpy old woman with her annoying dog."

In that case, the person at the door had to be one of the Finks from next door.

I braced myself for the worst and entered the narrow hallway that led to my front door.

A woman stood on the doorstep, her back to me as she surveyed the sunny front yard and the dirt path beyond. Her hair was blonde and curly, falling past her shoulders.

"Yes?"

"Oh!" The woman turned, and recognition sparked. It was Melanie—the poor dear who had been attacked a few days ago. "Hello," she said. "Ivy, right?"

Boo trotted to the front door to investigate the newcomer and gave her an appreciative lick on the knee. She petted him on the head, one hand grasping a dish covered in tinfoil. "And hello to you," she said.

"Melanie," I said. "Come in, dear. Come in."

She followed me into my little cottage, into the kitchen area.

"I was just making some coffee," I said. "Would you like a cup?"

"That would be lovely. Thank you." She set the dish down on the countertop. "I wasn't sure how to thank you for what you did the other day, so I baked you a lasagna. I hope you like lasagna? Or eat meat? Oh no, I didn't consider whether you eat meat or not." She picked up the dish. "That's so silly of me. I hope I haven't insulted you. I'll take it back."

"What? No, please don't. I love lasagna, and Boo loves meat. I'm sure it will be a hit with both of us."

Melanie released a relieved sigh and put the dish back down again. "Oh, that's good."

I poured her a mug of coffee, and she sweetened it with sugar before taking it in both hands. "Thank you so much," she said. "You've done so much for me already, I—"

"Anyone in my position would have done the same thing," I said.

"No."

"No?"

"I've been mugged three times since I moved to Somewhere," Melanie swallowed nervously. "And this is the first time someone helped me."

"I'm sorry to hear that."

"That last time, two men were walking by, and they acted like they didn't see a thing."

Anger bubbled up inside me, but it wouldn't help to get furious now. Not with this poor woman in my kitchen. Boo barked for the both of us, making it clear that he didn't approve of these shenanigans either.

"Somewhere has gone to heck in a handbasket," I murmured.

"I moved here to get away from it all," she said. "I didn't realize what I was getting myself into. I should've realized there was a reason the property prices here were so competitive. Moving into a house like that was a steal. They marketed it as a fixer-upper."

"It's a crime," I said. "Then again, everything in this

town is a crime nowadays." I gestured for her to come through to the living room. "What do you do for a living?"

"I'm a seamstress," she said. "I actually sew items for my online shop and ship them out. I make quite a bit of money from it, and it's fun to do, as well."

"That sounds great. I had no idea you could do that kind of thing nowadays. You sell the products online?"

"Yes. I make tea cozies, baby hats, socks, custom orders. All sorts of things. Sometimes, people want the strangest things, but if they provide the design, I can make it. It's fun." Melanie smiled. "When I was a girl, I wanted to be a fashion designer, but I realized that the high-paced, competitive environment wasn't for me."

She reminded me of a calmer version of my daughter. A little less confident, a little more timid. I found myself quite liking her—good thing she wasn't a suspect in the murder case.

"I decided that the best thing for me to do was to settle down in a small town and start a family. But now, I can't see myself starting one here."

"I wouldn't either, in the current 'climate,' so I don't blame you."

"I heard there was a murder at the museum this week. A woman was bludgeoned to death with a stone or something."

News always traveled fast in small towns and Somewhere was no exception. "That's exactly what happened," I said. "I've been fascinated by it."

"You have?"

I found it easy to talk to this young lady. It was a refreshing change of pace from the last couple of young people I'd met around Somewhere. "I've always been interested in true crime or murder mysteries. My favorite author is Agatha Christie."

"Oh, that makes sense."

"It does?"

"The bowler hat." Melanie gestured toward her head. "Hercule Poirot?"

"You're not far off," I said. "He's one of my favorite characters. But you can't beat a good Miss Marple novel, either. And, in my defense, my bowler hat is purple."

"Not that you need to defend yourself." Melanie laughed. "You could quite easily. I've never seen anyone smack another person over the head with an umbrella before. You really scared that mugger."

"Boo did most of the work," I said. "Did you report the crime to the police?"

"I tried."

"Tried?" Another spike of anger channeled through my core.

"When I reported it, they didn't seem interested in

what I had to say. They kind of shrugged it off. Like it was a regular thing to happen in town."

"Ah."

"I haven't heard from anyone since I reported it, but I guess that's okay. The last three times I reported, they didn't do anything either." Melanie sipped her coffee, her brows tipping inward as she considered what she'd just said. "I guess I just have to move away. There's nothing else I can do given the circumstances. If I stay, I'll only wind up getting in more trouble with lawless people, and I don't feel safe at night anymore. Not even with my doors locked."

"Just you wait," I said.

"Wait for what?"

"I'm going to clean up this town," I said. "Boo and I will clean up this town. You mark my words."

"But the police—"

As if on cue, a siren whooped outside. I rose from my seat and hurried to the window. A police cruiser was parked outside on the dirt road, a cloud of brown dust still surrounding it. The door opened, and Detective Darke stepped out wearing a pair of aviator sunglasses that had been hastily repaired with tape.

Fifteen

"TALK OF THE DEVIL, AND SHE WILL ARRIVE," I said.

Boo pattered over to join me, his tail alert.

"The police are here? Now?" Melanie pressed herself up from the sofa.

"Don't get up, dear. I'm sure this won't take long." A second door slamming brought my attention back to the police car outside. Another person had emerged from within, a young man with a jauntiness to his step. He was unfamiliar to me, but he wore a uniform, unlike Detective Darke, and a star on his lapel that told me exactly how he was.

The sheriff.

That was interesting.

Had Boo and I interfered so much that the sheriff had

come over from the neighboring town to pull us back into line again?

I left Melanie with her coffee and went to the front door. The rattling knock—obtrusive and irritable—came just as I reached it. I scraped the chain back and opened the door a crack.

"Can I help you?" I asked, eyeing Detective Darke through the crack.

Her half-repaired aviator sunglasses made her look even more ridiculous than usual.

"Mrs. Jackson," she said. "Mind if we come in?"

"Is this an official police visit?" I asked.

"Not technically."

"Have I done anything wrong?"

"Well, that's up for debate. You see—"

Boo barked at her, shoving his nose through the crack so that his lips pulled back to reveal little doggy teeth.

"Do you have a warrant for my arrest?"

"No, we—"

"Or a warrant to search my cottage?"

"No." Detective Darke grew red up and down her throat.

"Then I'm afraid I won't be letting you in," I said. "Given the fact that I have a guest, and this is an unannounced visit."

The young man, the sheriff, stepped past Darke with

an air of "I'll handle this." He put up an obsequious smile. "Good afternoon, Mrs. Jackson. My name is Sheriff Machito."

"Machito?" I asked. "Of the Flamin' Hot Machitos?"

Neither of them cracked a smile. A pity, since I'd thought that was a pretty good joke.

"I'm the sheriff of Nelson County," he said.

"You don't say," I said. "This little old county?"

"Yes, ma'am." The smile, which had briefly disappeared at my "in poor taste" joke, was back, pulling and twisting his features so that he seemed like more of a Cheshire Cat than a person.

Boo, of course, didn't like that at all. Cats were on the "no-lick" list and firmly on the "bite" one. He growled past his cute front teeth.

"And what are you doing on my front doorstep? I was under the impression that the sheriff's department was in the town over from ours."

"In Chester, ma'am," he said. "That's correct. I'm here to talk to you about, well, certain behaviors that have been occurring recently.

"Ah, of course," I said. "I've been meaning to contact you myself."

His eyebrows hopped upward in surprise. "You... have?"

"Yes, of course," I said. "The upward tick in crime in

the past few years is shameful. I've just been talking to a young woman who's been mugged a sum total of four times in the past couple of months. Can you believe that?"

"That's horrible," he said, opening his mouth as if he wanted to say something more before closing it again.

"Horrible, indeed. Even worse, if the crime continues here, I can't imagine it would look very good for you next time the election for the sheriff's position comes around. Don't you think?"

"I hadn't considered—"

"I'm sure people would be highly disturbed, for instance, to know that a detective and the sheriff himself are standing on an innocent woman's doorstep while murderers and muggers roam the streets unfettered."

"I—"

"But of course, you're probably here just to reassure me that you're taking things seriously in town, isn't that right?"

Boo barked through the gap in the door.

"I—"

"If I could get a word in, Sheriff Machito?" Detective Darke pulled the half-broke sunglasses off her face with a practiced ease that made her look even more ridiculous. She arched an eyebrow at me.

"How are you today, Mrs. Jackson?"

"I was doing a whole lot better before you arrived on my doorstep," I said.

"Are you always this...?"

"Brutally honest?"

Detective Darke cleared her throat, clearly unsure of what to say next. It was a funny thing, being older than most people. When you were an elder, people tended to tiptoe around you a little more. They forgave your grumpiness because they expected you were in pain or had a reason for being irritable. And they certainly didn't quite know how to handle you if you had anything irregular to say.

It was a game of mine, seeing how far I could push the envelope until people realized that I was a normal person who deserved the same respect as anyone else.

"We've had a call from an unhappy town resident," Detective Darke said. "It's our job to make sure her concerns are heard."

"Let me guess, the town resident in question was Mrs. Rosetta Stone."

"We can't confirm or deny who made the call to the sheriff's office," Detective Darke said.

Sheriff Machito made a garbled noise that could've meant darn near anything. My guess was he didn't want me to know that the Stones had a direct line to his office. I hadn't solved the murder yet, or cleaned up the town, but it gave me some comfort knowing that I had caused enough of a stir to bring the attention of the higher-ups in town.

They ought to be upset. They ought to pay attention to what was happening in Somewhere, because I would repeatedly ring the alarm until they did.

"We're here," Sheriff Machito said. "To make sure that everyone keeps the peace in Somewhere."

"Unfortunately, that's not up to me, Sheriff. You see, I doubt anyone will have peace until the murderer is caught. Or until people stop getting mugged in the suburbs. Seems to me like the local police need to patrol more or to start paying attention to the reports they receive at the police station."

"Now, listen here," Detective Darke said. "I'm only going to ask you this once. Stay out of our business and stay away from the Stones or you're in trouble, got it?"

"You forgot to say 'please,' Detective. And I haven't done anything to provoke the Stones."

Not that I needed to defend myself from these accusations. This whole visit was ridiculous, and the pair, who were both red in the cheeks, seemed to realize it.

"Please, will you stay out of trouble?" Sheriff Machito asked.

"Sheriff!" Detective Darke hissed.

She was ten years his senior, and he gave her a sheepish grin in response.

I considered the pair for a moment. "I politely decline your request." And then I shut the door in their faces, well aware that there wasn't a thing they could do about it.

Boo and I went back to the living room together and found Melanie exactly where we'd left her, looking flustered. "That was fantastic!"

"What was, dear?"

"The way you handled them. They didn't know what to do with themselves." She laughed, clapping her hands. "I want to be like you when I grow up."

I didn't have the heart to tell her that she'd wind up old and lonely if she chose that path.

Sixteen

Thinking deserved time and space and silence, and it was for those reasons that my favorite place to think was in the library. Particularly because Miriam allowed me to bring Boo inside—he was trusted not to pee on anything indoors, and he'd stuck to the rules. Thankfully. Dog pee on library books was a surefire way to lose my librarian friend.

I had arrived early the morning after my visit from Melanie and the pesky law enforcement officials, my library books tucked under one arm, and Boo on the end of his cute leash. I returned my books, found a private nook in the library, and sat down to consider what had happened to Cassandra Stone.

There were multiple possibilities, but the most solid connections had to be those people who were near or around the museum in the late evening hours on the night of the murder. A murder couldn't be committed without—

"Hey." The soft voice came from between the leaning bookcases nearest my side of the table.

Boo "ruffed" a warning.

"Hey, you. Mrs. Jackson?"

I searched for the source of the voice and found a pair of eyes peering out at me from a gap between two books. The person stood on the other side of the bookcase, barely visible.

"Who's that?" I asked. "And what do you want?" If it was the Queen of Rats... But she wouldn't be caught *dead* in a library, would she?

"I-It's Elsa. Elsa Fraggle. From Fraggle Rocks Jewelry."

I went over, positioning myself in line with the other side of the bookcase. If she wanted to practice subterfuge, I wasn't going to stop her. "What do you want?"

"I-I wanted to talk to you about—Look, I wanted to—"

"Go on."

Boo remained near my chair, watching with expressive border collie eyes, just in case I needed help.

"I wanted to thank you for what you did for me yesterday. Standing up to Mrs. Stone like that. That was really neat, and I, like, I wanted to say that you didn't have to do that, but you did, so that was really cool of you."

Ah, of course, the "Fraggle" word salad. I'd forgotten about it in the time since I'd last seen her.

"That's fine," I said.

"It's really not fine. Like, I know you stuck your neck out for me, and then I sort of chased you both off. I didn't want you to think that I was ungrateful. It was just a lot of pressure all at once, and I didn't know how to handle it, especially after everything I've been through in Somewhere with the people and the throwing rocks… And, yeah, with the police too."

"You saw the police again?"

"Detective Darke came by my place last night," Elsa said.

"Your place? The crystal shop?"

"Yeah. I live in the apartment above it."

That solved the mystery of where she stayed and whether she'd been in the area at the time of the murder. I'd mistakenly believed she didn't live near the crystal shop. "So you were at home on the night of the murder."

"I—Yeah. I was at home. I didn't do it, though. And I didn't even leave my bedroom. I just—I was around, but I —Yeah." Suddenly less word salad.

Then I had several people who were potential suspects in the area at the time—Joanie, the astronomer, who had claimed to briefly have visited the museum's exhibit, as well as Elsa, the murder weapon shop owner, and a homeless man.

"You could have thanked me any other time," I said. "Did you follow me here?"

Elsa smacked her lips. "I—Well, I didn't want anyone to see us talking."

"Why?"

"Because Detective Darke visited me and told me not to talk to anyone about anything or else."

"She threatened you?"

"Yeah. But, it's okay. I get it, like, that's what has to happen for her to solve the case, and the sooner she solves the case, the sooner I'll be able to carry on as normal. Or, you know, close up my store and move away from this town for good. I just want to get away from Rosetta Stone and her cronies."

"Who else has bothered you?"

"Cassandra used to." Elsa pressed a hand to her mouth like she'd said the wrong thing. "I don't know. I don't know. I just wanted to thank you. Things have been really weird. I'm not allowed to talk to you anymore, so I should go."

"Detective Darke can't stop you from talking to people," I said. "She has no right to."

"She doesn't?"

"No, she doesn't. She can't tell you who to talk to whether it's the cops or anyone else. Though, obviously, it would be better for you to have a lawyer present if you talk to the cops."

"A lawyer." Elsa gulped. "Can't afford a lawyer."

"Let's hope you won't need one."

"I—I keep hearing things."

This wasn't an issue I was willing to get into. I wasn't a licensed psychiatrist. "My dear, I wish I could help, but—"

"Not like that." Elsa pressed her forehead against the bookcase opposite, her green eyes growing round as an owl. "Not like I'm crazy." She let out a hysterical giggle. "I mean, I'm not crazier than any other person in this town, not that that's saying much after everything, but I'm not insane. I've been hearing things from the building next door."

"Such as?"

"Just noises. Which is really weird because it's an abandoned building. It scares me because what if someone is living in there, or what if it's the murderer? Or what if Cassandra Stone is in there, burrowing through the wall to get to me so that she can... I don't know, do something to me?"

"I'm not so sure about the last part."

"Yeah, okay, that was a little crazy, but still." Elsa

continued leaning in. Her forehead had to be killing her. "Listen, you said I could talk to you, so now I'm talking. I just—"

"You mentioned a homeless man yesterday," I said.

"Yeah, the homeless guy who lives on Artifact Street. I don't know his name, but he was hanging out around the museum quite a lot before it happened. I think the cops being around, like, chased him off. Don't blame him. Detective Darke scares me."

"Her bark is worse than her bite," I said.

Boo agreed loudly, and I shushed him, pointing to the sign against the wall calling for silence in the library.

"Do you know where I can find him?" I asked.

"Find him? Why would you want to find him? What if he's the murderer? What if—?"

"Don't worry about that," I said. "Where can I find him?"

"I think... Well, I saw him, like, circling the building a few times, so I think he might live out in the park. Or maybe he's the one making the noise in the abandoned building next—" Elsa stiffened, turning her head and listening hard. "I-I have to go. Bye." And then she raced off, leaving an air of fear and sage behind.

<h1 style="text-align:center">Seventeen</h1>

By this point in the week, I was certain Detective Darke, and the local police weren't taking the case seriously. The evidence was plain—they had jumped through hoops like performing collies at a dog show the minute Cassandra Stone had so much as blinked in their direction. And when I passed by the museum that afternoon, I found the seal on the doors to the museum had been removed, and Mr. Tilly's car was parked outside.

Could he be a suspect? He certainly had easy access to the museum as the person with the alarm code. But then, so had the Stones from his suggestion. It seemed that Cassandra could easily have broken in to continue her destruction from earlier in the evening on that fateful night.

Was she then followed? Or was it as simple as Mr. Tilly

finally taking exception and snapping?

I mulled the questions over, stopping outside the museum and peering up at the woman who sat behind the ticket counter, calmly paging through a newspaper.

Boo sat on my foot while I scanned Artifact Street.

It was true that the criminal would often return to the scene of the crime. Considering my presence at the museum lately, I was starting to look suspicious.

"Come on," I said. "The park."

Boo barked, startling the woman at the ticket counter in the museum. She gave me her most irritable look and shooed us off like we were peasants and she was The Queen.

The crystal shop doors were closed, and the abandoned building next door was silent as we rounded the corner and entered the overgrown park.

"Queenie" was nowhere to be seen, but I didn't trust she wasn't lying in wait in the long grass. Not that her presence would deter me from my questions or explorations.

The cluster of blankets and cardboard near the fence drew my attention. That looked like a makeshift home, as sad as it was, and another wave of anger washed over me. If the town had been better off, financially, then this wouldn't have happened to this poor man.

If the town had been in a better state, like it had been,

then my children would visit me. I would see my grandbabies.

Meanwhile, Cassandra Stone was launching crusades against small businesses and investing in the museum when the Stones could easily invest more of their money into the town in helpful ways. Into the local communities that had been affected by the closure of the plastic factory. Technically, that wasn't "on them" to do, but it was still a thought that lingered whenever I heard their names.

Boo barked at a man appearing from within the makeshift home against the fence.

The man froze.

He was balding, his eyes rheumy, his cheeks tan and sagging from long hours spent sitting in the sun.

"Don't mind me," he mumbled. "Just going about my business. Go on and use the park as you like. Just don't call the cops or nothing."

"I wasn't going to call the cops," I said. "In fact, they're the last people I'd call at this point."

"You and me both." The man gave a wheezing laugh, turning to leave the park.

"Wait," I called.

"Me?" He pointed at his chest with a gnarled finger.

"Yes," I said. "You. Can we talk?"

"Talk? You want to talk to me?" He stumped over, his pants starched with dirt and sunlight. "What for? 'Scuse my manners, but I don't usually get folks coming around asking to talk to me." He gave me a yellow-toothed grin.

"What's your name?"

His eyes grew a little watery. "Mason," he said. "You?"

"Ivy. This is Boo."

Boo wagged his tail at the man, tentatively. Boo gave people the benefit of the doubt until I told him they were enemies or until they did something to annoy him. That was why the Finks next door were such easy targets. They'd splashed him with, thankfully cold, water when he'd been having a fence-licking session with the chihuahua once. They'd been prime enemies ever since.

"Boo. Funny name for a dog."

"I know," I said. "But he came as a shock. Mason, do you think we could sit down together and talk?"

"You're not going to try to convert me to anything, are you? I'm right with God, just so you know."

I pressed a hand down on my bowler hat. "Actually, I wanted to talk to you about the murder at the museum."

"You don't look like a cop."

"I'm not. I'm just a nosy old woman."

"All right. That I can handle." He laughed.

"Or so you think. The park bench?" I gestured to it.

Mason led the way. He didn't smell great, of course, but he couldn't help that either, and it didn't matter to me. More importantly, he wasn't splattered with dried blood—unless he'd changed his clothes after "allegedly" murdering Cassandra. A possibility I had to confront.

We sat on the park bench together, a couple of feet apart, staring at the playground swing and the broken seat that hung motionless in the morning sunlight.

"I heard that you live around here, so I came to talk to you," I said. "You were outside the museum on the night that woman was murdered, weren't you?"

"Early in the evening. Fell asleep out there. Cold wind whipped through the park that night. The buildings in that street do a good job at breaking the wind."

So that was a yes. "And did you hear anything when you were out there?"

Mason stroked a dirty thumb over his mouth and turned a keen look on me then, a sharpness in his features that hadn't been there before. "You sure you're not a cop or nothing like that?"

"I'm not," I said. "I swear it."

"All right. Then yeah, I heard something. I woke up that night at about 09:30, see?" He rolled back both sleeves and showed several watches on each. There were dark scratches on his hands, which reminded me of the marks on Joanie's.

Defensive wounds? Two of the suspects had them now.

"Usually, I wake up a couple of times a night, so that

wasn't unusual or nothing, but this time, it was 'cos I heard a woman shouting."

My gaze drifted from the scratches to his serious, wizened face. "What was she shouting about?"

"Didn't quite make out the words, but she sounded real angry. And someone else was in there too, judging by the noise. I make it my business to mind it," he said, with a quick flash of his teeth. "So I left then. Went out to the park and settled in for the night."

"You didn't see or hear anything else?"

Mason broke eye contact, covering the watches on his arms. "Nothing."

"You're sure about that? There weren't any banging noises, or you didn't hear any other people?"

"Nothing," he repeated.

I fished around in my handbag for the granola bar I'd been saving for a snack and handed it to him.

"If you want it."

"Thanks." He took it. "This payment for the information or something?"

"Just gratitude," I said. "Stay safe, Mason."

"You too," he replied.

Boo and I had only walked off a few steps when his voice rose on the wind. "You're going to need to stay out of the park," he called. "People around here don't like folks who ask questions. I mean it, Ivy. Stay safe."

Eighteen

MASON'S WARNING STUCK IN MY EARS ALL THE way into the evening, while I ate the last remnants of my birthday cake, while I fed Boo, and while I idly spied on the Finks, putting my noggin to good use.

Options. Options. Options. So many options.

Cassandra murdered by an angry Mr. Tilly. But was there proof of his presence at the museum at 09:30 p.m.? I had arrived a half an hour later to discover the body and the crystal shards.

A sapphire missing, used as a murder weapon, stolen from Elsa. Or Elsa herself, covering her tracks by claiming her sapphire had been stolen and using it to murder Cassandra. Both options equally appealing.

Joanie Parker, in desperate need of work at the museum, there on the night and with scratches on her arms. Could she have argued with Cassandra, an old friend who might have been a frenemy? If so, why?

And then, of course, Mason, who had surely been in the area at the time and claimed he had heard a commotion, then threatened me in the next breath. But why? Why go to the trouble of murdering a woman with a stolen sapphire when he could run off with the sapphire and sell it and change his life?

The Queen of Rats kept popping into my thoughts—it could be because she had imposed on my personal space in the park, or it was a gut feeling about her being "bad." Though, I didn't need a "gut feeling" for that after the way she'd talked about the park and Somewhere.

The fading sunlight brought me out of my considerations to find Boo resting his head on my knee and peering up at me with concern. He huffed out a sigh, and I smiled at him.

"What about that abandoned building?" I asked him. "Should we go check that out?"

It was already late, which made it more dangerous out, but I wouldn't sit in place while the local detective did nothing but bow down to a rich family. And my curiosity had already gotten the better of me.

I clipped on Boo's leash, ensured that my pen flashlight was securely attached to my bowler hat, grabbed a cane from the stand next to the front door, and set off.

Twenty minutes later, after a peaceful walk down the dirt road and, past the library, into town, past the intersection of Main Street and Artillery Road, we entered the street that held the museum. The lights were on, the doors closed, and the pillars seemed like a mockery of the town. A relic in a time when people needed help more than they needed displays.

The crystal shop was silent and dark, and so were the upstairs windows, their curtains drawn, even though it wasn't even that late yet. Had Elsa gone into town? Or was she up there in the dark, plotting another murder?

Boo padded across the road, leading me toward the abandoned building.

It was just as dark as the crystal shop, and the front doors were boarded up. The windows were broken, but there was no way to enter without getting cut up.

"What do you smell, Boo?" I whispered.

We circled the building, searching for a way in. The crystal shop and the abandoned building were conjoined, with no alleyway between them. The back door was boarded up as well, so there were no means of entry there either.

A creeping feeling settled over me, and it occurred to me that it was dark and that someone might be watching from the park across the road. Mason. Or Queenie. Or the murderer if they weren't Mason or Queenie.

I led Boo back around the front of the building, and he snuffled at the base of the doors as if he could make out something before moving to the space beneath the windows and doing the same. He jumped up and let out a low growl.

A wind whipped past us, cold and bringing the vague scent of spring flowers, and whistled through the broken window, past wooden planks that had been tacked up haphazardly. There was just enough space to peer in between those planks and spy on what might be inside.

I checked the street both ways, ensuring that there was no one else around, and removed my pen flashlight from my hat.

I shone my beam of light inside, past the broken glass.

The walls beyond were sprayed with old graffiti. A half-broken staircase in the corner showed collapsed wood that was hazardous but didn't restrict a path to upstairs. The opposite doorway led somewhere deeper into the building, but I couldn't make out what was in there no matter how hard I tried.

Boo let out a muted bark, and I shushed him. "We don't want to get caught snooping around," I whispered. "Behave, dear."

And then, I returned to my study of the place. There were darkened shoe prints on the—

A wailing of sirens in the distance interrupted my

search, and I immediately clicked off the flashlight and led Boo away from the building, past the crystal shop.

Two police cars sailed into Artifact Street, tires skidding, and it would be remiss of me not to record that I'd been convinced they were here for me, specifically.

Much to my relief, and surprise, the cruisers drove past the abandoned buildings and took a right, heading toward the park. Boo and I chased after them, Boo barking his excitement at the commotion, and we peeked around the corner just in time to witness the arrest.

Detective Darke, her broken aviator sunglasses tucked into the top of her buttoned shirt, placed the "Queen of Rats" in cuffs behind the chain-link fence, cast into relief by the orange light of lamp posts along the street.

"You're crazy, pig. You've lost your darn mind. Don't you know who I am?"

"Ma'am, you have the right to remain silent. Anything you say can and will be used against you in a court of law. You have the right to speak to an attorney and to have an attorney present during questioning. If you cannot afford an attorney, one will be appointed for you. Do you understand, ma'am?"

"You idiot!" Queenie cried, holding stiff, even though her teeth were bared. "You think you can do this to me? I run this town! I—"

"Please state your name, ma'am."

"Queenie," she said.

"Your full name, please, ma'am."

"Maisie Barron," she grunted.

Not a very threatening name, after all.

"Miss Barron, do you understand your rights?" Detective Darke asked, guiding the Queen of Rats out of the park and toward the waiting cruiser. Another officer was on standby in case the detective needed help, following along and adjusting his belt and pants importantly after every other step.

"Yeah."

"In the back of the car, ma'am," the police officer said, opening the door and taking Queenie by the upper arm to force her inside.

"You pigs haven't even told me what I'm arrested for," she said.

The officer's eyes widened. Detective Darke's jaw worked by the light of a lamppost.

"I'm sure I did," Darke said.

"You didn't tell me anything," Queenie growled.

"I did, didn't I, Officer Bricks?"

"I didn't... uh, I didn't exactly hear, Detective." Bricks had a voice thick as molasses.

"Well, I *did* say it," Darke continued. "But since you need a *reminder*, I'll tell you that you're being arrested for the murder of Cassandra Stone. Anything you say or do can and will be used—"

"You already said that part," Queenie shrieked.

"Just put her in the car, will you, Bricks?" Darke strode back over to her vehicle without her usual pompous swagger while the officer fed an irate Queenie into the back of the car.

Boo and I backed up a few steps, but the cops weren't interested in us. They drove by, Queenie glaring out at the streets. Our gazes met as the cars cruised past, and she snarled at me, a hate-filled twisting of the lips and a promise that she would be out again. That I hadn't seen the last of her.

Nineteen

Boo went with me everywhere, even if it was to the grocery store to pick up a few items for the house. The company helped keep me focused on the present rather than the past, but that had become increasingly difficult of late.

The next morning was bright and full of flapping lips —people talking incessantly about the arrest of Maisie Barron, or Queenie, as some people called her. It seemed they weren't as familiar with her as I was. At least those shoppers in the grocery store weren't. I had a feeling that the folks from Sweetsville knew her well. The way she'd acted, I wouldn't have been surprised if she'd ruled the poorer suburb with an iron fistful of stolen dollars.

"Can you believe it?" A woman in the aisle over from mine asked.

I was in the middle of browsing the canned goods—Lucas Knott, the owner of the store, had a terrible habit of restocking cans in the wrong place, so that the canned peas were next to the preserves—but my ears perked up.

Boo whined and placed his paw on my foot, his claws scratching past the straps and onto my skin.

"I know," I mouthed. "I'm hearing it too."

"I can believe it," another woman said. "Don't you know who Maisie is?"

"No. I don't know her at all."

"She was a criminal. Grew up in Sweetsville, you know, and I heard they had her dead to rights. She was there on the night it happened, right in the museum."

"You're sure about that?"

"Of course. Would I lie to you, Desiree?"

The women moved off, still gossiping, and I took a can of peas and swapped it for the can of tomatoes beside it. The two had been switched, and it helped me get my thoughts in order, placing them in the correct spots.

After I was done, Boo and I collected the last of our groceries and went to the checkout counter at the front. Mr. Knott was servicing the two gossipy women at one, and the teenager with a permanently bored expression rang up mine.

I pushed my wheeled walker out into the street, pondering. "You know, you'll eat me out of house and home if you carry on like this. It's the second time we've had to come to the grocery store this week."

Boo whined-howled a talkative response.

"You're lucky you're so active," I said. "That's the only way you're keeping the weight off. I'm going to have to take you back to see Dr. Sarcosum again soon."

Boo barked at the name of the vet. Unlike other dogs and cats, Boo had a certain affinity for the vet—he liked the extra attention and that Dr. Sarcosum gave him two doggy treats at the end of a successful visit rather than one. The man, an intelligent one, had made a great deal of telling Boo that he was the only dog who got two treats because he was so well-behaved.

I had my suspicions about the truth in that statement, but it had worked on Boo and made vet trips far easier.

We started up the road, past that tempting bookstore, and a disheveled figure stepped out of the alleyway up ahead.

Mason came toward us, fast, glancing over either shoulder as he did.

He stopped a foot away. "Need to talk to you."

"What about?" I asked.

Queenie might have been arrested, but I didn't believe that Darke had all the evidence required to make the arrest in the first place. I was partly convinced that Darke had only arrested her on Rosetta Stone's insistence or under the pressure she'd placed on the police to find her daughter's murderer.

Another glance backward. "In private," Mason whispered. "Please."

"About what?" I repeated.

"About the Queen of Rats," he said. "She's been released."

I buried my astonishment. That silly Detective Darke had to have had absolutely nothing if the suspect had been released that quickly. How on earth had she gotten a warrant for the woman's arrest—unless new evidence had come to light that had absolved her of the crime.

"All right," I said. "Lead the way."

Mason turned back into the alley, and Boo and I followed, the end of my dog's leash tied to my walker. This was interesting—why would Mason have tracked me down. What could be this important that he would come to me instead of the police, unless he didn't trust the police at all.

Mason stopped behind a dumpster. "Here's fine."

I stood across from him, keeping a safe distance. Though he had seemed friendly enough during our chat the other day, I couldn't trust a stranger.

"Queenie was released?" I prompted.

He nodded.

"Why do you want to talk to me about that?"

"She was at the park the night it happened. The murder," he said. "Didn't tell you before 'cos I was scared she would find out. Queenie's got ears and eyes everywhere, doesn't she? Yeah, she does. I didn't know whether you was one of the ears and eyes, you know?"

Ah. That gave me one extra suspect.

One that had been arrested and released.

I had the feeling that Queenie's release might've been related to how she'd been arrested. And if that was the case, the Stones had to be absolutely furious about it.

"But I know you aren't with her," he said.

"How do you know that?"

"'Cos she put out a mark on you in Sewersville," he said. "You've got a target on your back. They're going to try to either get rid of ya or rob ya."

"Is that so?" The news should have sent a chill down my spine, but I found myself strangely unaffected by it.

"She's bad news, Ivy," he said. "And she'll come for you now that she's outta jail. She knows you were asking questions. Look, she's got a hideout at the old plastics factory, I think. But I don't know if it's a good idea to go out there. Not when she's around. She could hurt you."

"You're afraid of her," I said. "And you think she's actually the one that did it, don't you?"

He gave a slow nod.

"And you wish she would get put away for the crime."

"She's brought the entire town down. This used to be a good place. Sure, she's not all to blame, but she's a big part of the problem. Goes around threatening people. Robbing people. She was there that night. She was there. I just want her gone."

"Thanks, Mason," I said, reaching down to pet Boo. He had been dead silent since we'd entered the alleyway and hadn't even attempted to urinate on anything.

"Will you help, Miss Ivy?"

"I'll see what I can do." I bid him goodbye, then rolled my walker out of the alleyway and back onto the street, my thoughts bubbling with the possibilities.

The plastics factory was her hideout? Then I would have to go see what I could find—if there was real evidence, it would be where she spent most of her time.

Twenty

THE TOWN WAS IN AN UPROAR AFTER THE release of Maisie Barron, the Queen of Rats. Or, rather, the Stones and their wealthy friends were in an uproar. It seemed that they were the ones who had pointed the police in Maisie's direction, but I had an extra theory—Detective Darke was sloppy and had made several mistakes during and after the arrest.

Reading a suspect's Miranda Rights was usually done before questioning, not during an arrest. I was curious about the arrest warrant.

After our encounter with Mason, Boo and I returned to the cottage to drop off our groceries and have a quick snack before heading out again. No fence-licking and chihuahua-romancing for Boo today. We had a plastics factory to break into.

With a stop along the way.

The local gun store, Arms and Alarms, wasn't my usual haunt. I was a firm believer in the pen being mightier than the sword most times, but a lady needed a secondary form of protection that didn't involve barking and sharp teeth.

Besides, I didn't want Boo in harm's way if something went wrong during our trip to the factory.

"You heard the news?"

The guy behind the glass counter in the store wore a pair of glasses that slid down his nose repeatedly, so he had to keep pushing them up again.

"The news?" I asked.

"About that Cassandra Stone being murdered," he said, as he rang up my order of a can of pepper spray.

"I did."

"Just saying, the town's dangerous, more dangerous than it used to be. It's not safe for tourists," he said pointedly.

Had I been so cloistered that even local store owners didn't know who I was. I would've thought Boo had made a name for himself at least. "I was born in Somewhere," I said.

"Oh. Oh, well, shoot." The gun store clerk wiped off his hand and extended it over the countertop, nearly knocking the pepper spray over. "Name's Rick. Rick O'Hara. Nice to meet you."

"Ivy Jackson. This is Boo."

Rick smiled down at Boo. "Cute dog. They say border collies have the intelligence of the average eight-year-old child."

"Those must be some very smart eight-year-olds." I stroked Boo's soft forehead, and he wagged his tail at me.

"So, whereabouts do you stay in town?"

"Oh in a cottage past the library," I said. "It's peaceful out there. You must be doing good business in town lately after what happened."

Rick pulled a face. "You could say so. Of course, it's not *great* business because I have morals."

"Meaning?"

"I won't sell to Maisie or any of her crew. She came in here and tried to hustle me for money. Only took me telling her I was the one with the guns to get rid of her. You heard about her getting arrested?"

"And released."

"Mmhmm." Rick bagged the pepper spray for me and handed it over along with my change. "The Stones are throwing an adult temper tantrum over it. I've been listening to the police radio all morning." He gestured over his shoulder. "I heard they're going to pick her up again and bring her in for questioning today."

My heart lightened. If they did that, it might allow Boo and me an opportunity to get into the plastics factory without Queenie finding out. Either way, we had to try.

We said goodbye to Rick and started our journey toward the plastics factory. I opted for the long way around, avoiding the local park where Mason had made his home. Then crossing the train tracks into Sweetsville, I approached the plastics factory from the east.

The homes in Sweetsville were run down compared to when I'd been down here years ago. Several of the buildings were abandoned, but not boarded up, and those homes that were occupied had chipped paint or overgrown gardens, broken fences, and cracks in the plaster of the houses themselves. Many of the houses looked perilous to live in, and the more I walked along the cracked sidewalk, the angrier I became.

It wasn't fair that people in Somewhere had to live like this. Surely, there had to be something I could do to help.

Boo and I passed an open plot of land that was barren, dotted with garbage, an old mattress lying out in the middle of the space, springs poking out of it here and there. Boo gave an enigmatic whine.

"Nothing we can do yet, Boo. Let's focus on the murder first." I wasn't usually biased, but even I had to admit that getting Maisie into prison and off the streets would be a step in the right direction when it came to straightening out the town.

The old plastics factory loomed up ahead, the spires silent and rusted, the chain-link fence surrounding it cut in places or gone altogether in others.

Boo and I stopped opposite it, surveying the area.

A warehouse flanked one portion of the property, and graffiti was sprawled across the wall—an image of a rat wearing a crown, a piece of cheese beside it.

"My guess is that's where we're headed," I said.

Boo and I lingered, waiting for any sign of activity. All was silent—for now.

We headed across the street and through one of the openings in the fence. "Watch your paws," I whispered. "This place is a health hazard."

On one hand, the town needed the plastics factory for jobs and money, on the other, factories were polluters. My theory was that if we cleaned up the town enough, Somewhere would seem more attractive to potential investors. People's lives would return to normal. They would—

I reached the door and pressed it open with the toe of my boot, my finger poised on the top button of my pepper spray. If anything happened, Boo and I would be ready for it.

The inside of the room was empty of activity, but the evidence of people living in the warehouse was evident.

There were makeshift beds, pictures tacked to the walls, and weapons resting against a hodgepodge of tables and chairs.

At one end of the vast space, with its cracked floor and old, leaning metal shelves, sat a "throne" that had been cobbled together. A desk to one side of it drew my eye.

"We have to be quick," I whispered. "Before they get back."

I had no idea how many "rats" Queenie had, but I didn't want to find out.

A worn map lay across the top of the desk, and there were several pins arrayed across it. One of them had been driven into the map right on top of the spot where my cottage had been built. Another was pegged into the train tracks at a specific spot, a note beneath it reading "May 20th, 10:00 p.m." I snapped a picture of the map with my phone—today was the 20th—then continued my search.

The desk drawers were empty except for an old picture. The glass cracked, but the image beyond still clear. I brought it out, twisting it by the meager light that arced through the small windows along the very top of the warehouse wall.

Garrett Stone had his arm around a man in a warehouse manager's uniform—assumption on my part, but the guy looked important. And familiar. Too familiar.

The recognition hit me a second later. "Mason," I whispered.

It was the homeless man who had tipped me off about the noises on the night of the murder. And about the Queen of Rats.

Two sets of heavy footsteps sounded behind me.

"Well, well, well, what do we have here?"

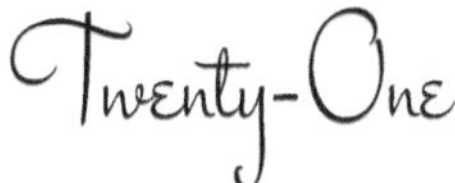

Twenty-One

Boo growled and prepared himself to attack. I turned, my finger still on the trigger for the pepper spray, expecting to find Mason and the Queen of Rats waiting for me. But it wasn't Mason at all.

Queenie stood side-by-side with a man I didn't recognize—he was tall, with a large black bump on his forehead and bloodshot eyes.

"Hey!" he shouted. "Hey, that's the lady! That's the lady and her stupid mutt."

Queenie nudged the guy beside her. "Shut up, Rooney."

"But that's the one I told you about, Queenie. She beat me over the head with an umbrella. I was just trying to shake a lady down, and that dog—that dog minced my ankle."

Boo growled a promise that he'd do it again.

"Idiot," Queenie hissed. "You just identified yourself."

Rooney licked his lips nervously, his fingers creeping upward to the bump on his forehead. "Sorry."

Queenie turned her attention toward me. "You've come to the wrong place if you're looking to stay safe," she said. "Mrs. Ivy Jackson."

I held completely still, making a mental plan of escape. Panic wasn't in my vocabulary at the moment—when things like this happened, a coldness descended upon me, and a certainty that I would get Boo out of there no matter what.

We were closest to the throne and furthest from the distant exits on either side of the warehouse.

"Oh, I know who you are," Queenie said. "I've been watching you, even when you don't realize it."

"Except when you were in jail, I assume," I replied.

Queenie's cheeks grew red. "You're gonna talk to me like that? Here, in my house?"

"I told you, boss, she's crazy. She beat me over the head with an umbrella."

"That's not something I would be advertising, Rooney," Queenie snapped. "You got beaten up by an old woman and her annoying dog."

Boo bark-growled at Queenie. I kept my grip firm on

the end of his leash so he wouldn't do anything that would lead to harm—for himself, of course.

"You're going to regret ever coming here." Queenie took a step toward us.

"Yeah." Rooney's addition.

"And I'm going to make sure you never interfere in my business again."

"Yeah."

"I'm going to punish you and your dog."

"Yeah."

"Rooney, would you stop saying that?"

"Yeah," he said, then clapped a hand over his mouth. "Sorry, boss. I mean no."

Queenie glared at him.

"I mean, yeah?" His voice had gone squeaky.

These two were clowns. Darren, who probably thought I had lost the few marbles I had left knocking around in my noggin, would've cracked their heads together and gone on with his day. Unfortunately, I was neither as tall nor as strong as my husband had been.

I pulled the end of Boo's leash, indicating that he got behind me, and then aimed my pepper spray at the pair. I unleashed a stream of pepper spray first at Queenie, and then at Rooney. The pair yelped and almost immediately doubled over.

Rooney let out unholy shrieks and clawed at his eyes

while Queenie bent at the hips and grasped her knees before falling to them on the concrete.

I didn't stick around to witness the after-effects. I directed Boo toward the exit at the back of the warehouse, running as fast as my sore hip would let me.

Twenty-Two

PERHAPS IT WASN'T THE BEST TIME TO SEEK OUT new clues, but my rationale was that Queenie and her lackey would be indisposed for quite some time, thanks to the strength of the pepper spray. It had been my best purchase to date, and I would have bet that Rick from the gun store would have been in awe of who had been the pepper spray's first victim.

With the necessity to stay calm and in control for Boo's sake gone, the shakes had started on our way through Sweetsville. I was forced to take deep and even breaths so I wouldn't pass out after the altercation, and we crossed the train tracks and found the park without incident.

Boo and I sat down on the park bench—or rather, I sat

on the bench while Boo plonked down on my foot—and stared off into space for a few moments.

"We should call the police," I said, then dismissed the thought right after. "Who am I kidding? They wouldn't do a darn thing. Not without evidence. Especially not after what happened with Detective Darke's botched arrest."

Boo barked in agreement.

I stroked his head, still clinging to the tube of pepper spray and his leash, my heart pounding out a rhythm. I had to admit, then, that I had never felt this alive. Or I hadn't felt this alive in a long time, at least.

I had taken on Queenie and her goon and lived to tell the tale. And I had retrieved information relevant to Cassandra Stone's murder, even if one of those pieces of information had come in an unexpected form.

The picture of Garrett Stone and Mason.

I couldn't be entirely certain that Mason had been a warehouse manager, but he had to have been a higher-up in the company if Garrett had taken a picture with him. Especially one that was so "cozy."

Which left me with a motive for Mason to have murdered Cassandra. It very well could have been that Mason wanted to strike back at Garrett in revenge, but that didn't explain his choice of a murder weapon, nor the fact that he hadn't run the minute the deed had been committed. The police in town wouldn't have noticed him missing—they only cared when it was to chase a homeless person away.

"But wouldn't he have kept the sapphire?"

Mason had also pushed me in the direction of Queenie, and I hadn't found any evidence in the plastics factory that had indicated she'd been directly involved in Cassandra's murder. Only Detective Darke's arrest and Mason's testimony claimed she'd been in the area that acted as evidence.

My gaze fell on the small home Mason had made against the fence in the park.

It appeared empty. Had Mason stayed in town this morning, perhaps avoiding any fall-out from my visit to the plastics factory? Had he sent me there, hoping that Queenie would get rid of me and thus "his problem?"

I rose from the bench, bringing Boo along with me toward Mason's makeshift home.

It was mostly made of cardboard, but a few sheets of corrugated metal leaned against the fence to provide shelter from the elements. Somewhere was miserable during the winter, and empathy rose within me before I could squash it down.

This man might be the murderer.

I peered into his little home. There wasn't much—a

collection of blankets, a few trinkets around the outside of the space, a bottle of water, and a small bowl beside it. No sapphires or shards of sapphire, and definitely not bloodied clothing or even pictures of the Stones or his time at the plastics factory.

A rustling from the blankets brought a muted bark from Boo.

I eased him with petting.

A small feline face peered out from between the blankets. A ginger cat, just into its gangly adolescent years, meowed at me, intrigued by my presence in its home. Boo stiffened, and I tightened my hold on the end of his leash.

Boo wasn't an unfriendly dog, but he drew the line at cats. His only feline acquaintance was the Finks' cat next door, and it was a cretinous animal that liked to jump on him when he was taking afternoon naps in the yard, its claws extended.

The cat arched its back, purring, then traipsed over to the bowl next to the bottle of water. It bent and started drinking down sips.

Boo and I backed away, leaving it in peace.

Ideas and connections formed in my mind, but I didn't discuss them with Boo yet. I needed to get us home and find my trusty tape recorder—usually on me at all times in my tote bag—and work through this verbally. I had opted not to bring my bag along for the plastics factory operation, just in case things turned sour. A good decision, as it turned out.

Boo and I soon left the park behind and went home. The walk was longer than usual, partially because we were both still shaken up, and partially because I was exhausted after the quick jog from the plastics factory. I wasn't cut out for rigorous physical activity like that anymore.

At home, I firmly locked the cottage's front door, checked the windows were secured, and then dished up a large slice of cake for myself and a bowl of food for Boo.

We ate in silence.

The sugar went a good way toward helping me overcome my shock. I drank sips of water in between, then finally fixed myself a coffee and retrieved my phone and tape recorder from my tote bag.

A message notification flashed on the screen.

"Hey, Mom! I miss you. Just wanted to send some love. Here's a picture of us and the kids."

My beloved daughter Brianna had attached an image of their little family together.

I smiled, tears welling in my eyes at the sight of them all so happy together.

I dialed her number, desperate for encouragement after the week Boo and I had been having.

"Mom?"

"Hi, Bri," I said. "How are you?"

"Oh, busy as always. Did you get the photo I sent you?"

"I sure did! It's lovely. I can't wait for you all to come visit so we can take pictures together. You know, I'm telling you, Somewhere's going to be safer than it used to be."

"Mom, you know safety wouldn't keep me from coming to see you," Brianna said.

My heart leaped. "Then you'll—"

"Things are just a bit complicated at the moment. They're busy. Once the kids are a little older and used to car rides, maybe." Brianna swallowed. "Besides, we're planning a big move in July, so that's something we've got to take into account."

"Where are you moving to?"

"Minnesota."

My joy crashed to the floor. "But that's further away."

"I know, Mom. I'm sorry I didn't tell you sooner. We've just been so busy, and I didn't want to disappoint you."

"Don't be silly, Bri. You couldn't disappoint me. As long as you're happy, that's all that matters."

I forced myself not to get emotional. I didn't want to guilt trip my daughter for living her life as she wanted to.

"You're amazing, Mom. I'll call you back later, okay? I've got to run."

"Love you."

"Love you tons!" And then she was gone.

I put the phone on the coffee table and stared at it for a while before I burst into tears.

Twenty-Three

I didn't usually make a habit of sitting in the dark as the sun set, but this was the second time in a week that I had found myself in the living room, staring out of the window at the purple dusk, with Boo's head in my lap. Emotion had clogged my throat on and off since the phone call with my daughter. I hadn't heard from my son since his message on my birthday, and the world, tonight, seemed darker than it had since Darren's passing.

It was during moments like these I missed his presence even more sorely. A stray thought about the comfort he might have given me if he'd been here was enough to send me into tears all over again.

Boo whined and wagged his tail, desperate to comfort me even though I stroked him.

It was completely dark out when I finally rose to close the curtains and switch on the lights in my living room.

Boo followed me around, licking my stockings and trying to encourage me.

I removed my bowler hat and put it on the rack beside the door, then made myself some green tea and lowered myself into the chair again.

"We're not going to dwell," I said.

And then proceeded to dwell, regardless. I had my tape recorder in my lap, but nothing could will me to use it at the moment. I sipped my tea, eyes streaming, and occasionally reached for Kleenex to dab away the tears.

"Always have each other, won't we Boo?" I petted him. "Assuming we don't get attacked by Queenie and her gang of—"

A knock rattled the front door, and Boo barked.

I put down my cup of tea, dabbed my cheeks, and went to it. I swept the bowler hat back onto my head.

"Hello? Who's out there?"

"It's Melanie."

I opened the door for her, ushered her inside to a cacophony of welcoming barks from Boo and a quieter amount of licks, then locked the door firmly behind her.

"I hope I'm not imposing," Melanie said in between laughing at Boo's antics. She spotted the seriousness of my expression. "Mrs. Jackson? Are you all right?"

"It's been a rough week," I said. "Come on in. I hope you didn't walk here."

"Oh no, I brought my car. I got it fixed up by a mechanic in town." Melanie hesitated. "I can leave if this is not a good time. I wanted to stop by and check in on how you were doing."

"Me? Why?" I gestured for her to take a seat at the kitchen table. "Hot chocolate?"

"That would be lovely."

The green tea certainly wasn't working—a little extra sugar might do the trick.

"And some cake," I said.

"I love cake. Was it someone's birthday?"

"Mine," I said.

"Oh, happy belated birthday! I'll have to get you a gift," Melanie said.

"That's not necessary. You gave me that delicious lasagna."

"You enjoyed it?"

"It was fantastic," I said. "I've got your dish here somewhere." I rooted around for it and brought it down. "Thank you very much."

"You're so welcome. I like cooking when I'm not working on a new design." Melanie paused. "Is this a bad time?"

"No, no, not at all. I think this might be the best time for a visit, actually," I said.

"I hope I'm not imposing. It's just... you're the first friend I've made in town, and you seem like a rational person."

"Thank you," I laughed, and it felt good to laugh at that moment. "I pride myself on being rational, and you're not imposing at all."

I fixed us both cups of hot chocolate, and we ate our cake together and laughed. Melanie talking about the last few days and a pervading feeling of loneliness that I was all too familiar with.

"What about your family?" I asked. "I'm sure your mother or father would love to hear from you."

"Unfortunately, I lost my mother a few years ago." She took a sip of her hot chocolate, squeezing her eyes closed for a moment.

"I'm so sorry to hear that."

"Thank you," she said. "And I never knew my father, unfortunately. Or fortunately. I think he was a bit of a flake. So, all-in-all, it's nice to have someone to talk to."

"I agree."

And it was nice not to talk about anything serious for a while. We joked around about the antics of Boo with the chihuahua next door, and Melanie told me about her experiences with her neighbor, who stayed up late and made strange squawking noises at all hours of the night.

"I didn't know whether to report it or not," Melanie said. "Until he left the curtains open one night, and I saw he was doing what looked like an interpretive dance in front of his computer. I think he's recording videos for YouShare."

"That had to be quite the sight."

Eventually, our conversation faded, and Melanie had to head out. Once she was gone, a warmth settled in my chest.

So, I couldn't change the town to what it had been before, but I could still make a difference. For myself, for Boo, and for the others who lived here.

I grabbed my tape recorder, inspiration taking hold of me in the silence.

"We have four suspects. One might effectively be ruled out, thanks to the evidence. Another is very likely, but more clues are needed to prove she was at the scene. The other two are tenuous. I need to investigate them thoroughly."

Boo barked, adding his testimony.

"Primary target must be someone who has the murder weapon, who was near the area, and who has a motive. Joanie Parker lives with the Stones. Elsa Fraggle has been acting strangely and complaining about the abandoned buildings. Three courses of action present themselves. The train tracks, the abandoned building, the Stone house."

I checked the time on my phone. It was almost time for the clandestine meeting at the train tracks that had been noted on Queenie's map.

Was I really going to go down there and face her again? Fear should have kept me from doing it, but there was so much at stake. A murder mystery, an entire town hanging in the balance, and people like Melanie, who were good and pure and deserved more than what Somewhere had to offer at the moment.

"Boo," I said. "Grab your leash. We're going for a walk. But we're going to have to be very quiet. Do you understand?"

Boo whined a response and ran to get his leash.

Twenty-Four

BOO AND I TOOK THE DIRT ROAD PAST THE library and into town together in the dead of night, Boo moving like a shadow. I had opted to put on a black houndstooth coat and a pair of black leather gloves to go with my bowler hat in the hopes that it would keep me hidden when we reached the train tracks.

Apart from crossing them earlier in the day, it had been a long time since I'd seen the train tracks. There wasn't a station in Somewhere, but the tracks ran right through the town, onto the next town. Boo and I took the route in relative quiet, Boo barely stopping to sniff anything along the way for once.

I noted that the museum lights were on and the doors closed, the crystal shop in darkness, and the abandoned building next door was quiet. We slowed as we passed it, but there were no noises inside.

Interesting. That could suggest one of two things, but I wasn't invested in either of the outcomes yet.

I checked that I had my cell phone firmly tucked into my coat pocket in case I needed it, the tape recorder in the other.

The moon was hidden behind a blanket of clouds, only occasionally peeking its face out to shine lights on the ground. My thick-soled shoes crunched gravel underfoot as we approached the tracks. Boo slowed before I did, and we ducked behind a tree hidden among the tall grass near a bend in the track.

I checked the time on my phone and then the picture of the map I'd taken, though it took me a minute to bring it up. Was it just me, or were phones unnecessarily complicated?

We were ten minutes early but at approximately the right spot. Boo lay down in the tall grass to wait while I hovered behind the tree, feeling out of place. I could almost hear Darren chuckling at my antics. He would never have let me do this, though.

Guilt washed over me. I hadn't been adventurous enough in the last years of his life. But I hadn't realized that he wasn't going to be around for much longer, and losing my children had taken more of a toll on me than I had cared to admit at the time. The world had become a little less colorful after my daughter had gotten married.

Our jobs had been done, and then there was nothing but Darren and me left to deal with a big house. The sale had gone through fast, the cottage had seemed perfect, so close to the library, and then—

The crunch of footsteps approaching silenced my introspection.

A figure appeared on the train tracks, coming from the direction of the plastic factory. They were hunched over, skittish, and stopped a short distance from my hiding spot. I didn't dare move, thanking the heavens that I was in the tree's shadow and nearly pushed up against it.

Another few minutes later, a second person appeared, this one instantly recognizable as Queenie herself.

I brought my tape recorder out and clicked the button on itself, breathless at the sound it might make.

They were close, but I wasn't sure if the recorder would pick them up. I just had to hope.

"You did what I asked you to do?" Queenie's voice rang out, commanding and powerful.

Boo didn't make a sound but lay flat in the grass, unmoving. I prayed that he would stay that way.

"Yeah. I did what you asked, though I didn't like doing it. She seems nice enough." It was Mason.

"Nice guys finish last," Queenie said ominously. "Didn't anybody ever tell you that?"

Mason didn't reply.

"So, you're ready to do it then?" Queenie asked.

"Do it? Me?"

"Who else do you think would do it?" Queenie laughed. "I can pay you well enough. Here's what you're gonna do. You're gonna go to her house, tie her up, take everything you can that's valuable." She paused to sniff and muttered under her breath.

"What's the matter?"

"Darn pepper spray," she said. "Nothing. Forget about it. Listen to my instructions."

"I don't want to do it."

"You'll be paid, and you'll do it. I want everything cleaned out of her house. Everything. You know where she lives. The target is Ivy Jackson."

"I know all of that, but I'm still not doing it," Mason said.

"You've got a death wish."

"I've got the opposite," Mason said. "Don't want to end up sniffling like you, do I? She pepper sprayed you."

"I can do much worse than that," Queenie replied. "And I will if you don't do as I say. While you're at it, beat her up a little bit. If the dog gets in the way, you know what to do."

"I don't hurt animals," Mason said.

"You do it." Queenie had drawn closer to him, that much I could see. "You do it, or I hurt you. I don't need no old lady moving in on my turf. This is my town, you hear me." She grabbed hold of the front of Mason's clothing and dragged him toward her. "You worthless piece of trash. You should be lucky I ask you to do anything." She pushed him back, and he stumbled and almost fell.

"I won't do it. She's a nice old lady."

"And you're a dead man walking," Queenie said.

Mason straightened to his full height. "I know you were there," he said. "The night that the girl was murdered in the museum. I saw you in the park."

"You idiot," Queenie said. "You saw me in the park, which means I didn't murder her."

"That doesn't matter. They'll believe me if I tell them. I can get you locked up. That's where you belong, Maisie. In prison after everything you've done to this town. In prison right along with your ma."

"Why, I'll—" She took a step toward him.

Something in Mason's posture changed. He took a step toward her, stronger and less afraid than before. "I'm not doing anything for you, hear me? I'm not going to live my life afraid of a woman like you."

Queenie trembled on the spot, either with rage or fear.

"Then what are you gonna do when I send my people for you next? You'll really pay the price for that old bat?"

"Not right," Mason said. "Not right. None of it's right."

"Babbling fool."

"Done plenty wrong in my life. Hurt people. Lost my family when the plastics factory closed. But I won't... won't keep doing the wrong things anymore. You leave me alone, hear me?" Mason took a step forward. "You leave me alone, or I'll go to the cops and tell them everything I know about you."

"They wouldn't believe you."

"But they'll believe Mrs. Jackson," Mason said. "They'll believe her. So you'd better watch yourself. Got it?"

Queenie let out a rage-filled shriek before turning on her heel and disappearing back the way she'd come, the gritty crunch of ballast marking her passage. Mason let out a breath and deflated before leaving in the opposite direction.

Twenty-Five

THE NEXT MORNING WAS A BRIGHT, WARM SPRING day, and it felt almost as if the mental fugue had lifted, and I could function again. I fed Boo a healthy breakfast, fueled myself with a bowl of bran, and prepared for the day, doing a light purple lip to match my bowler hat while my border collie watched from the bedroom door, his furry butt pressed to the jamb.

"Boo," I said, with a swish of my lipstick tube, "We can't change the past. But maybe we can change the present after all."

The thought had come to me after what Mason had said to Queenie last night. He had worked for her, but he had double-crossed her and ultimately proved to me that she had an alibi for the murder.

Of course, that wouldn't stop me from dropping off

the recording of what had been said with the police. Hopefully, it would get her off the streets for a while. Planning to "hurt" an old lady was a criminal offense, as was a robbery. And overhearing her talk about Boo had unleashed an anger in me that I'd never experienced before.

Boo and I took a leisurely stroll into town, stopping to drop off my library books before talking to the police about the tape and reporting the crime. Melanie had been entirely correct about how lackluster they were—it felt as if they weren't taking what I had to say seriously.

Which, of course, in turn, made me even more determined to solve this case. If I did it when the police couldn't, that was bound to be embarrassing for them.

"And after that's happened," I said to Boo, as I inserted a fresh tape into my tape recorder, "we'll talk to the newspaper about what happened. They'll have no choice but to change then."

Boo barked his agreement. We avoided Artifact Street this time and headed past the police station and toward the upper-class suburb where the Stones lived. Their mansion was situated on a wide tarred lane that wound past trees and neatly kept parks—nothing like the other side of town.

Apparently, their safety and comfort was taken seriously.

A lot of the homes on Lily Lane were similar in that they had high stone walls, a few of them with electric fencing on top to keep out the criminals. If Queenie had caught sight of these targets, she would have constructed a plan to break in and rob them blind.

But judging by the quality of her "gang"—the bruised and inept Rooney being the example—she wouldn't get very far.

"That's why we have to take away her power before she gets too strong, Boo," I said. "We're lucky that she hasn't managed to gather too much of a following just yet. Although, Mason was afraid of her."

Boo's paws pattered along the sidewalk. He paused to lift his leg against a tree along the side of the road, and I held my tape recorder in hand and hit the button on it.

"Mason, the homeless person, cleared of the crime. Queenie, cleared of the crime. Both witnessed each other in the park, and Queenie would have no reason to lie in a private conversation with Mason, especially when she had no fear of him. Which leaves just two suspects. The strange crystal shop owner, who I'm convinced is hiding something and the elusive astronomer who has been keeping to herself at the Stone residence. Our next stop has to be the Stone residence to talk to Mrs. Rosetta Stone or Mr. Garrett Stone. Or Joanie herself. We have to gather more information about her to determine whether she was at the museum during the right time period."

I clicked off the tape recorder.

The intercom beside the Stone's front gate was encased in hard, clear plastic, so I had to reach a finger through a tiny hole to press the buzzer.

A crystal clear voice came down the line. "Good morning," a woman said. "May I help you?"

"I'm here to talk with Mrs. Rosetta Stone," I said.

"I'm afraid the lady of the house isn't here at the moment. She's attending a very important charity event."

"All right, then, may I talk to Mr. Garrett Stone?"

"Mr. Stone is in the middle of a—"

"Who's that?" A gruff voice in the background.

"I'm not sure, Sir, I—" The chatter cut off as the housekeeper or maid removed her finger off the intercom button. I waited patiently, Boo sitting beside me, idly scratching at his collar, the leash clinking.

"Who is this?" An irritable man came through the speaker.

"Hello," I said. "My name is Ivy Jackson. I was hoping to talk to Garrett Stone or, failing that, Joanie Parker."

"Joanie—" Another dead quiet as the intercom cut out.

"Hello?"

"Stay there," the man said. "I'm coming down to the gate."

I stepped back from the intercom, slipping my tape recorder into my handbag. I pressed my hand to my bowler hat as a strong wind swept down Lily Lane. The gates were wrought iron and provided a view of the triple-story mansion at the end of a sweeping lawn. The driveway wound toward it, flanked by hedges, a few of them blooming flowers.

A gardener worked on a bush nearby, chopping off the flower heads with a ferocity that was a little startling.

Five minutes later, a figure appeared at the end of the grand driveway, striding toward us. Mr. Stone had a powerful gait that matched the suit he wore. He reached me and stopped, his Italian leather loafers so polished they reflected the morning sunlight.

"Ivy Jackson," he said. "My wife has told me about you."

"That's good to know."

"Yeah, it's safe to say your reputation precedes you." Garrett sounded impressed rather than angry about my last conversation with his wife. "Rosetta has a bad habit of going off on crusades. She has a lot of energy that's almost always directed incorrectly. I've sent her off to a charity event in New Orleans."

"That's far away," I said.

"Absence makes the heart grow fonder," Garrett said. "Especially when that absence allows me to get my work done. I must admit, I'm intrigued by you. The fact that you managed to get under my wife's skin so effectively is impressive. Why do you want to talk to me about Joanie Parker of all people?"

"She was friends with your daughter," I said, noting that Mr. Stone didn't look that distraught about Cassandra's passing.

"Ah, yes. Was. In high school. Cassandra had similar 'energy' issues as her mother," Garrett said. "Good spirit, incorrect direction." He rubbed his brow, and his features sagged for a moment, the roughness fading into sorrow. He cleared his throat. "Joanie and Cassandra. They were inseparable at one point."

"I got the impression that they had been arguing recently."

Garrett paused to consider it. "Well, yes. According to my wife, there was a good reason for that. Cassandra didn't want Joanie to work at the museum."

"She didn't?"

"Cassandra was a complicated girl. She loved her life, and she didn't want anyone interfering with it, especially not an old friend from high school. She felt that Joanie working at the museum would interfere with her peace."

From what I'd seen and heard of Cassandra, peace had been the last thing on her mind.

"So she stopped Joanie from getting the job at the museum?"

"That's correct."

"Then why did Cassandra ask Joanie to live with you?" I asked.

"With us?" Garrett brushed off his suit sleeve. "What gave you that idea?"

"She's not living with you?"

"No, of course not. The girls stopped talking years ago. The argument between them was the first time Joanie and Cass had interacted since high school."

Twenty-Six

THE REVELATION REQUIRED MORE RESEARCH. Joanie was looking more and more likely to be the killer, but there wasn't enough proof yet. And there were loose ends that needed to be tied. Boo and I took a brisk walk away from the mansion after Garrett Stone had grown bored with our conversation and returned to his work.

My opinion of the man was that he was out of touch with reality. Out of touch with the town. But that he wasn't inherently evil, that I could gather so far. First impressions could be deceiving, though, as I would later find out—but that is a tale for another time.

Boo and I navigated back to Artifact Street for what I hoped would be the last time in a while. At this rate, we might as well have started renting the space next door to the crystal shop—our ultimate destination.

Fraggle Rocks Jewelry was open today, thankfully, but the commotion inside indicated that all was not well.

I tapped my knuckles on the glass front door, peering into the dusty interior, past the square sign that read **OPEN** hanging in the door.

Elsa was inside, and she froze at the sight of us, her pink hair frazzled and standing out in every direction like she'd been electrocuted. She had an armful of crystals, an open crate filled with packing material at her feet. Her mouth formed a little "o" at the sight of us.

I tried the front door and found it unlocked. I dropped the end of Boo's leash and allowed him to bound inside. He barked at Elsa excitedly, jumping around her and wagging his tail. It was as if he was trying to tell her we were almost done with our investigation.

"Good morning, Miss Fraggle."

"Hello, Mrs. Jackson." She delivered the crystals into the packing material inside the crate. "What are you d-doing here?"

"I thought I would come by to talk to you. Check in and see how you are doing. You know, it's been one heck of a week."

"Y-Yeah."

I had to use my noggin. Why was she shaky? What was she hiding?

I walked along a row of empty shelves toward the crate

at Elsa's feet. The jewelry that had hung against the wall behind the counter had been hastily removed—a few pieces hung askew, half off their hooks.

"You're leaving town?"

"W-Well, yes," she said.

"Why is that? Surely, not because of Rosetta Stone."

Elsa pressed her lips together and nodded. "Yeah," she said. "I have to, like, leave because of her. Definitely." And no other information after that.

For a woman who usually loved to blab, she was suddenly quiet.

I let that awkward silence linger between us, my gaze fixed on her face. Sweat trickled down one cheek, making a track from her temple to her chin. "C-Can I help you with something?" Elsa asked.

"Like I said, we were just visiting. Do you need us to help you pack?"

Elsa gulped. "T-That's okay. I think I'm just going to take some time alone. You know, like, I mean, like, Rosetta's been stressing me out."

"Did she verbally attack you again?"

"Uh... Yes! Y-Yeah, she came by this morning and started yelling at me again."

A lie, given that we'd heard from Garrett Stone, he'd sent his wife off to a charity event in New Orleans. And unless Rosetta had unlocked a new level of evil and was able to teleport across time and space, I had a tall tale on my hands.

Boo let out a low growl. He didn't like being lied to either.

I patted my leg for him to join me, and he backed away from Elsa.

"So, you've been packing because you've given up on selling your jewelry here?" I asked, ready for the final reveal of my knowledge. I had been keeping one piece of information close to my chest all week, hoping it would be relevant.

"That's right." She walked around to the back of the counter and took down a few of the tiaras that hung there.

"Ah. You know," I said. "I have a beautiful engagement ring. I keep it on my dressing table in its velvet-pillowed box. It's the same box my husband used to propose to me years ago."

"That's lovely." Elsa had relaxed a little.

"And the ring, it's so beautiful. I think you would like it, anyway. The ring has a one-carat diamond and two little sapphires on either side of it."

"Cool."

"And that's why I know that sapphires, expensive and durable sapphires, do not chip or flake easily," I said. "It's also why I know that the murder weapon, the sapphire that was stolen from your shop, couldn't have been a real sapphire at all because it flaked with such ease."

Elsa froze, the tiara trembling in her grasp.

"And it's also why I know that the murder weapon wasn't stolen afterward or kept, but likely disposed of or hidden." I studied her reaction. Boo waited, quiet and alert. "So, now, my question has to be, why would you tell me that the sapphire stolen from your shop was priceless? And why are you packing up your store with great haste just after the only other suspect in the case has been released?"

Elsa let out a choked noise.

"Unless you had something to do with the murder?"

"I-I didn't do anything to Cassandra."

"Then why did you lie about the sapphire?"

Elsa shushed me frantically, and Boo barked in protest —no one was allowed to shush me except for him and vice versa. "P-Please, keep your voice down."

"Why? What are you hiding, Miss Fraggle?"

"I—" She gulped. "I think they're listening to us next door."

"Who's listening to us?"

"The insurance company people," she hissed. "I don't want them to know that I'm leaving. I—"

"You committed insurance fraud," I said.

Another furious round of shushing and barking.

"I know they have people following me and listening in on my conversations. Look, I was desperate. I know that the sapphire was stolen, and I'm pretty sure that they aren't going to find it because, well, the police, like, haven't been great at finding the murderer."

"Ah, so you figured you would claim from the insurance and expect them to pay," I said. "You lied about how much the sapphire was worth."

"They won't pay out," Elsa whispered. "They've been listening to me." She tapped gently on the wall connected to the abandoned building next door. "So, I have to leave before they track me down. I know I did the wrong thing, but I was poor. I was desperate. Please, you can't, like, tell anybody. You c-can't."

I sighed. What else would this week throw at us? "I'm afraid that you're going to get in trouble no matter what you do. You claimed that you had a huge chunk of sapphire that was used to knock somebody out. That wasn't plausible from the start."

"No, you see, that's not what I did with the insurance company. I claimed it was a small pure sapphire rather than a huge one," Elsa said. "I'm not that stupid."

"Ah. I see."

"What do you, like, think I should do?"

"You want the brutal truth?" I asked.

Elsa gave a slow and teary-eyed nod. "Tell your insurance company the truth. Apologize. Talk to the police."

Fraggle's crestfallen expression showed that was the opposite of what she'd wanted to hear.

I tipped my bowler hat to her and exited the crystal shop. It was still morning. We had a long wait ahead of us for our plan tonight.

Twenty-Seven

Boo and I spent the day finalizing our plans for the evening. It was of the utmost importance that we had everything in order, from our escape plan, to our evidence-gathering techniques. By eight o'clock that evening, I had tucked a spool of Darren's old fishing line into my bag, along with my leather gloves, two sturdy cable ties, my tape recorder, and my handy, almost empty, tube of pepper spray. In addition, I had my bowler hat with my pen flashlight attached and had spent a significant portion of the late afternoon figuring out how to record audio with my phone in case the tape recorder didn't work.

Boo was outfitted with a black leash—a new addition to his repertoire of fancy leashes—and had been well-fed and watered for our mission.

I slipped on my houndstooth pea coat and checked my

bowler hat was in place. My bag strung firmly over one shoulder, and then we set off into the purple dusk as we had earlier in the week. This time, our destination wasn't the train tracks.

The twenty-minute walk brought us past the museum and to the abandoned building right as darkness had fallen.

I detached my pen flashlight from my bowler hat and checked the windows of the abandoned building as I had previously. They were boarded up as they'd been before, but I had a theory.

Elsa believed that someone was listening in on her from next door. She thought it was the insurance company.

I happened to think she was half-right.

And if there was a person hiding in the building, then they had to have easy passage inside. It wouldn't be through these windows.

Boo and I circled the building again and found the back door boarded up as it had been earlier in the week.

"Use your noggin," I murmured.

I drew my pen flashlight over the sides of the boards, searching for clues. I pressed my gloved fingers to the boards and pressed on them. They wiggled slightly, and Boo made a soft whine of encouragement, snuffling at the base of the obstruction.

It was only after his pawing that I noticed the very fine outline at the bottom of the boards. What looked to be a trap door, just big enough to crawl through, had been cut into the wooden planks. Whoever had been entering and exiting the building had been doing so on all fours and had carefully replaced the planks each time they did.

"This is not going to be easy on my joints," I muttered, lowering myself onto the top step—concrete and remarkably uncomfortable. I sat side-saddle and wormed my fingers around the edge of the wooden trap door. It popped free with a little elbow grease.

Boo was raring to get inside, but I restricted him with a pat on the end and a stern look. I set the board to one side and directed my pen flashlight inside. The hallway was empty, free of dust, and led toward the broken staircase in one corner.

"All right," I whispered. "This is our cue."

I scooched my way through the hole with as much dignity as possible—which was to say, none at all—and called for Boo. He scooted through with much more enthusiasm and waited patiently for me as I pulled the board trap door back into place.

I pushed myself upright, grunting a little at the effort. I would certainly regret this in the morning, but what choice did I have?

Boo and I progressed through the house, the old wood

creaking underfoot, and then made our way up the stairs. Boo jumped over the gaps in the stairs with ease, avoiding splinters and danger like he'd been born to do this. I took my time, grasping the balustrade in places—there were marks on it displaying that someone else had used it in a similar fashion. Repeatedly.

At the very top of the stairs, a splodge of dark *something* marked the end of the railing. I didn't touch it but removed my phone as quietly as I could and took a picture. I fished the pepper spray out and used my pen flashlight to navigate the darkened upstairs hallway. The boards were so creaky. If there was someone up here, they would surely hear me coming.

That was what the pepper spray was for.

Two rooms took up the space on the top floor, with two doorways on either side of the hall. The first was empty, the floor bare and ruined, the struts on display.

The second room…

"Ah," I said. "It seems we've found it. Boo, darling, wait over here."

Boo, obediently for once, seated himself beside the door to wait for my investigation.

The room had a makeshift bed in the corner, the sheets neatly made. Beside it was a small LED lamp that was currently off. A suitcase, open to reveal clothing, sat beside that. And then there were books. Books on astronomy and science, textbooks with the markings of a university.

I took pictures of everything with my phone, taking great care to go over to the pile of rags discarded in one corner. I moved them with my gloved hands carefully. They were spotted black with what I suspected was blood spatter, and in the very center of the pile, a large, blue rock, chipped on one side, had been hidden. A fake jagged sapphire.

We had every bit of evidence we needed.

I recorded everything with great care, picture after picture. Videos.

My temptation to call 911 was great, but I held back. The truth of the matter was I had my doubts about Detective Darke responding to a call to this abandoned building. She was resistant to evidence and input, as had been the indication when she'd arrived on my doorstep with the sheriff.

I had to deliver, not only the evidence, but the murderer herself.

Which meant Boo and I would have to stay there and wait for the murderer to return to the scene of the crime. Two options were available when I'd first arrived—that the murderer would be present and I would pepper spray them, or that they wouldn't be there and it would be time to set the trap.

"Are you ready for the setup?" I asked Boo.

He stamped his paws onto the wooden boards, giving me the go-ahead.

I sent up a quick prayer, thinking of Darren and hoping he was watching over me as we did this. I needed every bit of help I could get.

We made quick work of laying the trap, Boo overseeing me and sniffing around in the hallway intermittently. After everything was arranged, I placed the bloodied clothing and murder weapon back as I'd found it and called Boo into the room to wait with me.

Joanie Parker was out, roaming the streets or finding work since Mr. Tilly had opted not to give in when it came to the job, but if she slept here, she would have to return soon enough, and when she did, we would be ready and waiting for her.

I brought out my tape recorder.

"The suspect has been hiding in an abandoned building all along. A clear upstairs view from the half-boarded window down into the street overlooks the park. This indicates that Joanie must have seen both Mason and Queenie in the area. It also means I'll see or hear her approach. Now, all we have left to do is wait for her arrival and execute the plan. We need all the luck we can get."

Boo placed a paw on my foot as if to tell me that everything would be all right.

Twenty-Eight

Hours passed in silence. Boo snoozed beside me in the dark, my pen flashlight off and clipped back into place on my bowler hat. My gaze was glued to the window and the view of the park and the street outside. An hour ago, Mason had returned to the park with a small bag of what looked like cat food and disappeared into his hutch against the fence. Since then, it had been completely silent.

The tension built steadily in the old abandoned building. An odd bang or creak rang out and there was the occasional noise of the TV from Elsa's apartment next door. Apparently, she'd opted not to make a run for it after all.

At quarter to midnight, a figure turned the corner into the street.

Joanie Parker, her brown hair tied back into a glossy

ponytail, paused outside the abandoned building and looked up and down the street, back into the park, and around the corner, before bending and quietly detaching the trap door.

I nudged Boo with the toe of my boot. "Action time," I murmured.

His bright eyes peered up at me and then focused on the doorway.

I had to hope that the plan would work. I sent up another prayer as Joanie's steps creaked up the staircase and entered the second-floor hallway.

I held my breath as she approached the door.

The next sequence of events happened at such speed I could do nothing but act rather than think.

She entered the room and tripped over the fishing line I had tied across the front of the door. She fell flat on the floor with a curse before rolling onto her back. Boo let out a fantastic bark and dove toward her pinning her to the floor.

I brought out my pepper spray, my pen flashlight switched on and aimed at her, and let out a targeted stream. It hit Joanie directly in the eyes. She screeched.

Quick as I could, I ran to her side while Boo lay on top of her body.

I grabbed her ankles and slipped a cable tie over them while Boo terrified her with growls and snaps near her face.

The wrists were more difficult, as she had pressed her hands to her eyes, but I managed.

Joanie Parker screamed. She tried kicking her feet and bringing her hands to her face again, but it was too late for her. We had captured her thoroughly. I called Boo away, so that he wouldn't get hurt somehow in the process of detaining our suspect, and then exited into the hallway, bringing my phone out.

"All right, Boo," I said. "I think we can finally call 911."

THE FOLLOWING MORNING, BOO AND I WERE summoned into the mayor's office. I was stunned that we had received an invitation and even more taken aback when I realized that he was an individual who appeared to care but was working against the tide of corruption in the town and making little headway.

Mayor Franklin was skin and bone, in his mid-forties, and looked as if he was one coffee away from snapping at anyone who got on his bad side. He wore a t-shirt and a pair of jeans as he drew us into his office and didn't seem to mind when Boo invaded his personal space for a good old-fashioned butt-sniffing. He fended him off sure, but he wasn't offended, and that counted for a lot.

"Thank you for coming down to see me, Mrs. Jackson," Mayor Franklin said. "Please, take a seat."

The chair in front of his desk was the same as the one behind it. I sat down. "Nice to meet you, Mayor."

"And you," he said, taking his place. The desk wasn't oversized either. "I wanted to personally thank you for putting your life in danger yesterday. As I understand it, you were the one who caught Cassandra Stone's killer."

"If I hadn't caught her, no one else would have," I said. "I've got a bone to pick with you, Mayor. The police are not doing their job to clean up this town. I shouldn't be the one solving anything, and you know it."

"I do," Mayor Franklin said. "And I'm not going to pretend like everything's okay. I've long been suspicious that things had gone foul at the Somewhere Police Department, but your interference and citizen's arrest of the murderer has given me the ammunition I need to actually make headway into changing things."

"That's good news."

"I've started that headway by making sure that the most recent rash of crimes reported are taken seriously, and I've asked the Chief of Police to report to me directly regarding open cases and how they're progressing." He shifted papers across his desk. "That includes the one you reported recently. A Miss Maisie Barron was arrested this morning on the evidence you've given. As was a man named—"Another shuffling of papers. "Rooney Grant."

Triumph whooped through my stomach. "That's wonderful news."

"I want to assure you that I'm going to be on top of this," Mayor Franklin said. "You've made waves over the past few days, Mrs. Jackson. A ripple effect that has traveled through Somewhere. People want things to improve. All we can do now is look to the future and do the work."

"Thank you," I said. "That's exactly what I needed to hear."

Look to the future. It would be bright if we worked together, of that much I was certain.

Twenty-Nine

In the months after Joanie Parker's arrest, small things about Somewhere began to change. The police did as the mayor had promised and started cleaning up the town at a faster rate, people greeted each other more often, and morale and sentiment rose as a whole. I was the recipient of a commendation from the Mayor, a small award that sat on my kitchen counter to be admired every morning. A sign that I had done something good. Something to remedy the mistakes I had made along the way in my life—one of those being a lack of self-care and care for those around me.

To be accepted into the community was a wish I hadn't realized I had until Melanie and Miranda began visiting with frequency. Until they started asking me to help organize small events in town.

They were all steps in the right direction. If we could take control back, if we could make Somewhere a place to live and love and raise families again, I would consider myself a happy—

Barking started up outside my cottage, and I set my pen down, shaking my head at the interruption.

Boo and the Chihuahua next door—I had learned her name was Isabelle—were licking each other through the fence again.

I left my journal and pen behind, grabbed my bowler hat from the hatstand, the keys to my cottage, and a walking stick, then stepped out onto the front porch.

"Boo," I called. "Come get your leash. We're going for a walk." We only had an hour before we had a lunch date with Melanie and Miriam. A new cafe had opened in the spot where the Fraggle Rocks Jewelry store had been, and it looked promising.

Boo gave the fence one last excitable lick before dashing inside, and fetching his leash. He brought it to me, and I clipped it onto his collar.

Isabelle let out several yaps, begging to come along with us, and a door slammed in my neighbor's cottage.

Mr. Fink, large, in charge, and with a red rash where his beard used to be, emerged from his home, scratching under his chin irritably. "Isabelle. Isabelle, get away from the darn fence."

"Good morning, Mr. Fink," I said. "How are you today?"

Mr. Fink grunted at me.

"Good, I take it." I closed my front door and took hold of Boo's leash.

"You taking him out for a walk?"

"I'd be happy to take Isabelle along, too," I said.

Mr. Fink pulled a face like I'd suggested he shave his legs too.

"Suit yourself." I started down the pathway, Boo barking twice at Isabelle before coming along with me.

We strolled down the long dirt road, Mr. Fink's gaze following us, as well as Isabelle's excitable barks.

Boo and I took the dirt road past the library but opted to turn away from the grocery store and the road that led toward the museum. We took our old, favorite route, and as we drew ever closer to the old house, our old house, my heartbeat grew faster.

"Almost there," I said to Boo, the keys to the cottage tucked into my moist palm. "Almost there."

We turned a corner and there it was.

The old house.

And there was a truck parked outside. A moving van.

I pulled up short.

The person we'd sold the house to, years ago, had never

moved in, but had allowed it to fall into disrepair. It seemed they had sold it on again.

I watched, a strange warmth unfolding in my chest as a car pulled up in the driveway. A young woman emerged from behind the wheel. Her husband got out of the passenger seat. The two grinned at each other over the top of the car.

The back doors swung open, and two young children, two girls with their hair in matching pigtails, and wearing cute puffy blue skirts with polka dots, darted out of the car.

"I'm choosing my room first!" the first girl cried.

"No fair! I'm choosing. I'm choosing! Natalie, slow down!" The second girl raced after her sister. Shrieks and giggles followed as the girls darted past two men carrying an armoire and sped into the house.

The front door had been fixed, the yard had been mowed, and the windows repaired. There was still work to be done, but it was an amazing transformation.

Emotion clogged my throat. Boo whined and sat down on my foot.

The mother and father shut their car doors and walked toward the house together, arm-in-arm, joy radiating from them.

I waited until they were inside before walking past the house, tears wetting my cheeks and a smile parting my lips.

"Boo," I said, pressing a hand to the white heart shape on his forehead. "It looks like we're going to have to find a new walking route after all."

He barked a happy reply, and we continued on down the sidewalk together into a brighter future.

Thank you for being one of the first to read Ivy Jackson's adventure! Boo and Ivy will return in the next book in the series, The Incorruptible Ivy Jackson and the Cafe Corpse, coming to the website, rosiepointbooks.com at the end of April! Please turn the page to find out how to grab your launch week goodies.

Craving More Cozy Mystery?

If you had fun with Ruby and Bee, you'll, love getting to know Charlie Mission and her butt-kicking grandmother, Georgina. You can read the first chapter of Charlie's story, *The Case of the Waffling Warrants,* below!

"Come in, Big G, come in." I spoke under my breath so that the flesh-colored microphone seated against my throat picked up my voice. "What is your status?"

My grandmother, Georgina—pet name Gamma, code name Big G—was out on a special operation. Reconnaissance at the newest guesthouse in our town, Gossip. The reason? First, she was an ex-spy, as was I, and second, the woman who'd opened the guesthouse was her mortal enemy and in direct competition with my grandmother's establishment, the Gossip Inn.

Who was this enemy, this bringer of potential financial doom?

A middle-aged woman with a penchant for wearing pashminas and annoying anyone who looked her way.

Jessie Belle-Blue.

It was rumored that even thinking the woman's name summoned a murder of crows.

"I repeat, Big G, what is your status?"

"I'm en route to the nest," my grandmother replied in my earpiece.

I let out a relieved sigh and exited my bedroom, heading downstairs to help with the breakfast service.

In the nine months since I had retired as a spy, life in Gossip had been normal. In the Gossip sense of the term. I'd expected that my job as a server, maid, and assistant would bring the usual level of "cat herding" inherent when working at the inn. Whether that involved tracking down runaway cats, literally, or providing a guest with a moist towelette after a fainting spell—tempers ran high in Gossip.

What was the reason for the craziness? Shoot, it had to be something in the water.

I took the main stairs two at a time and found my friend, the inn's chef, paging through her recipe book in the lime green kitchen. Lauren Harris wore her red hair in a French braid today, apron stretched over her pregnant belly.

"Morning," I said, "how are you today?"

"Madder than a fat cat on a diet." She slapped her recipe book closed and turned to me.

Uh oh. Looks like it's time for more cat herding.

"What's wrong?"

"My supplier is out of flour and sugar. Can you believe that?" Lauren huffed, smoothing her hands over her belly while the clock on the wall ticked away. Breakfast was in two hours and Lauren loved baking cupcakes as part of the meal.

"Do you have enough supplies to make cupcakes for this morning?"

"Yes. But just for today," Lauren replied. "The guests are going to love my new waffle cupcakes, and they'll be sore they can't get anymore after this batch is done. Why, I should go down there and wring Billy's neck for doing this to me. He knows I take an order of sugar and flour every week, and I get it at just above cost too. What's Georgina going to say?"

"Don't stress, Lauren," I said. "We'll figure it out."

"Right." She brightened a little. "I nearly forgot you're the one who "fixes" things around here." Lauren winked at me.

She was the only person in the entire town who knew that my grandmother and I had once been spies for the NSIB—the National Security Investigative Bureau. But the news that I had helped solve several murders had spread through town, and now, anybody and everybody with a problem would call me up asking for help. A lot of them offered me money. And I was selective about who I chose to help.

"I'll check it out for you if you'd like," I said. "The flour issue."

"Nah, that's OK. I'm sure Billy will get more stock this week. I'll lean on him until he squeals."

"Sounds like you've been picking up tips from Georgina."

Lauren giggled then returned to her super-secret recipe book—no one but she was allowed to touch it.

"What's on the menu this morning?" I asked.

Lauren was the boss in the kitchen—she told me what to do, and I followed her instructions precisely. If I did anything else, like trying to read the recipe for instance, the food would end up burned, missing ingredients or worse.

The only place I wasn't a "fixer" was in the Gossip Inn's kitchen.

"Bacon and eggs over easy, biscuits and gravy, waffle cupcakes and... oh, I can't make fresh baked bread, can I?"

"Tell her I'll bring some back with me from the

bakery." Gamma's voice startled me. Goodness, I'd forgotten about the earpiece—she could hear everything happening in the kitchen.

"I'll text Georgina and ask her to bring bread from the bakery."

"You're a lifesaver, Charlotte."

We set to work on the breakfast—it was 7:00 a.m. and we needed everything done within two hours—and fell into our easy rhythm of baking and cooking.

My grandmother entered the kitchen at around 8:30 a.m., dressed in a neat silk blouse and a pair of slacks rather than the black outfit she'd left in for her spy mission. Tall, willowy, and with neatly styled gray hair, Gamma had always reminded me of Helen Mirren playing the Queen.

"Good morning, ladies," she said, in her prim, British accent. "I bring bread and tidings."

"What did you find out?" I asked.

"No evidence of the supposed ghost tours," Gamma said.

We'd started hosting ghost tours at the inn recently, so of course Jessie Belle-Blue wanted to do the same. She was all about under-cutting us, but, thankfully, the Gossip Inn had a legacy and over 1,000 positive reviews on Trip-Advisor.

Breakfast time arrived, and the guests filled the quaint dining area with its glossy tables, creaking wooden floors, and egg yolk yellow walls. Chatter and laughter leaked through the swinging kitchen doors with their porthole windows.

"That's my cue," I said, dusting off my apron, and heading out into the dining room.

I picked up a pot of coffee from the sideboard where we kept the drinks station and started my rounds.

Most of the guests had gathered around a center table in the dining room, and bursts of laughter came from the group, accompanied by the occasional shout.

I elbowed my way past a couple of guests—nobody could accuse me of having great people skills—apologizing along the way until I reached the table. The last time something like this had happened, a murder had followed shortly afterward.

Not this time. No way.

"—the last thing she'd ever hear!" The woman seated at the table, drawing the attention, was vaguely familiar. She wore her dark hair in luscious curls, and tossed it as she spoke, looking down her upturned nose at the people around the table.

"What happened then, Mandy?" Another woman asked, her hands clasped together in front of her stomach.

Mandy? Wait a second, isn't this Mandy Gilmore?

Gamma had mentioned her once before—Mandy was

a massive gossip in town. Why wasn't she staying at her house?

"What happened? Well, she ran off with her tail between her legs, of course. She'll soon learn not to cross me. Heaven knows, I always repay my debts."

"What, like a Lannister from *Game of Thrones*?" That had come from a taller woman with ginger curls.

"Shut up, Opal," Mandy replied. "You have no idea what we're talking about, and even if you did, you wouldn't have the intelligence to comprehend it."

The crowd let out various 'oofs' in response to that. The woman next to me clapped her hand over her mouth.

"You're all talk, Gilmore." Opal lifted a hand and yammered it at the other woman. "You act like you're a threat, but we know the truth around here."

"The truth?" Mandy leaned in, pressing her hands flat onto the tabletop, the crystal vase in the center rattling. "And what's that, Opal, darling? I'd love to hear it."

"That you're a failure. You sold your house, left Gossip with your head in the clouds, told everyone you were going to become a successful businesswoman, and now you're back. Back to scrape together the pieces of the life you have left."

"Witch!" Mandy scraped her chair back.

"All right, all right," I said, setting down the coffee pot

on the table. "That's enough, ladies. Everyone head back to their tables before things get out of hand."

Both Opal and Mandy stared daggers at me.

I flashed them both smiles. "We wouldn't want to ruin breakfast, would we? Lauren's prepared waffle cupcakes."

That distracted them. "Waffle cupcakes?" Opal's brow wrinkled. "How's that going to work?"

"Let's talk about it at your table." I grabbed my coffee pot and walked her away from Mandy. The crowd slowly dispersed, people muttering regret at having missed out on a show. The Gossip Inn was popular for its constant conflict.

If the rumors didn't start here then they weren't worth repeating. That was the mantra, anyway.

I seated Opal at her table, and she pursed her lips at me. "You shouldn't have interrupted. That woman needs a piece of my mind."

"We prefer peace of mind at the inn." I put up another of my best smiles.

Compared to what I'd been through in the past—hiding out from my rogue spy ex-husband and eventually helping put him behind bars when he found me—dealing with the guests was a cakewalk.

"What brings you to Gossip, Opal?" I asked.

"I live here," she replied, waspishly. "I'm staying here while they're fumigating my house. Roaches."

"Ah." I struggled not to grimace. Thankfully, my cell phone buzzed in the front pocket of my apron and distracted me. "Coffee?"

"I don't take caffeine." And she said it like I'd offered her an illegal substance too.

"Call me if you need anything." I hurried off before she could make good on that promise, bringing my phone out of my pocket.

I left the coffee pot on the sideboard, moving into the Gossip Inn's spacious foyer, the chandelier overhead off, but catching light in glimmers. The tables lining the hall were filled with trinkets from the days when the inn had been a museum—an eclectic collection of bits and bobs.

"This is Charlotte Smith," I answered the call—I would never get to use my true last name, Mission, again, but it was safer this way.

"Hello, Charlotte." A soft, rasping voice. "I've been trying to get through to you. I'm desperate."

"Who is this?"

"My name is Tina Rogers, and I need your help."

"My help."

"Yes," she said. "I understand that you have a certain set of skills. That you fix people's problems?"

"I do. But it depends on the problem and the price." I didn't have a set fee for helping people, but if it drew me away from the inn for long, I had to charge. I was technically a consultant now. Sort of like a P.I. without the fedora and coffee-stained shirt.

"My mother will handle your fee," Tina said. "I've asked her to text you about it, but I... I don't have long to talk. They're going to pull me off the phone soon."

"Who?"

"The police," she replied. "I'm calling you from the holding cell at the Gossip Police Station. I've been arrested on false charges, and I need you to help me prove my innocence."

"Miss Rogers, it's probably a better idea to invest in a lawyer." But I was tempted. It had been a long time since I'd felt useful.

"No! I'm not going to a lawyer. I'm going to make these idiots pay for ever having arrested me."

I took a breath. "OK. Before I accept your... case, I'll need to know what happened. You'll need to tell me everything." I glanced through the open doorway that led into the dining room. No one looked unhappy about the lack of service yet.

"I can't tell you everything now. I don't have much time."

"So give me the *CliffsNotes*."

"I was arrested for breaking into and vandalizing Josie Carlson's bakery, The Little Cake Shop. Apparently, they found my glove there—it was specially embroidered, you see—but it's not mine because—" The line went dead.

"Hello? Miss Rogers?" I pulled the cellphone away from my ear and frowned at the screen. "Darn."

My interest was piqued. A mystery case about a break-in that involved the local bakery? Which just so happened to be run by one of my least favorite people in Gossip?

And when I'd just started getting bored with the push and pull of everyday life at the inn?

Count me in.

Want to read more? You can grab **the first book** in *the Gossip Cozy Mystery series* on all major retailers.

Happy reading, friend!

Paperbacks Available by Rosie A. Point

A Burger Bar Mystery series

The Fiesta Burger Murder

The Double Cheese Burger Murder

The Chicken Burger Murder

The Breakfast Burger Murder

The Salmon Burger Murder

The Cheesy Steak Burger Murder

A Bite-sized Bakery Cozy Mystery series

Murder by Chocolate

Marzipan and Murder

Creepy Cake Murder

Murder and Meringue Cake

Murder Under the Mistletoe

Murder Glazed Donuts

Choc Chip Murder

Macarons and Murder

Candy Cake Murder

Murder by Rainbow Cake

Murder With Sprinkles

Trick or Murder

Christmas Cake Murder

S'more Murder

Murder and Marshmallows

Donut Murder

Buttercream Murder

Chocolate Cherry Murder

Caramel Apple Murder

Red, White 'n Blue Murder

Pink Sprinkled Murder

Murder by Milkshake

Murder by Cupid Cake

Caramel Cupcake Murder

Cake Pops and Murder

A Milly Pepper Mystery series

Maple Drizzle Murder

A Sunny Side Up Cozy Mystery series

Murder Over Easy

Muffin But Murder

Chicken Murder Soup

Murderoni and Cheese

Lemon Murder Pie

<u>*A Gossip Cozy Mystery series*</u>

The Case of the Waffling Warrants

The Case of the Key Lime Crimes

The Case of the Custard Conspiracy

<u>*A Mission Inn-possible Cozy Mystery series*</u>

Vanilla Vendetta

Strawberry Sin

Cocoa Conviction

Mint Murder

Raspberry Revenge

Chocolate Chills

<u>*A Very Murder Christmas series*</u>

Dachshund Through the Snow

Owl Be Home for Christmas

9 781776 432592